WHAT ARE THE ODDS?

WHAT ARE THE ODDS?

by Jacob Vos

Writers Club Press
San Jose New York Lincoln Shanghai

What are the Odds?

Writers Club Press
an imprint of iUniverse, Inc.

For information address:
iUniverse, Inc.
5220 S. 16th St., Suite 200
Lincoln, NE 68512
www.iuniverse.com

Some of the characters, events, and places herin are based on reality. Names have been changed to assure anonymity. Also, be sure, the thoughts and ideas of the main character are not the thoughts and ideas of myself. If you decide to get mad at someone, make it him, not me.

ISBN: 0-595-21974-8

Printed in the United States of America

This book is dedicated to all of those who are kind enough to go out of their way to read it, as well as to all of my friends and family that have helped me along the way.

Acknowledgements

THANKS TO:

My parents, without whom none of this would be possible. Christine, for offering me a respite from everything bad in my life. My best friend Ryan, for guilting me into finishing me this. To Rose, Keirsa, Zoë, Aaron, Paul, Pete, Derek, Erik, Josh, and countless others for inspiration. To my extended family for their support. To the people and city of Milaca and it's public schools. To the book and movie Hi-Fidelity for their inspiration. To Erickson's World Famous Hi-Way Café for sustaining my writing. To everyone who has read this, for better or for worse. To Pilot and Uni-Ball pens for providing me with my tools. To Blink-182, Sum 41, A New Found Glory, the Dave Matthews Band, and others for providing music to write to. To my publishers, my editors, and finally, to you.

CHAPTER 1

*I*t is the worst New Year's Eve of my entire life. Am I having a wonderful dinner while watching the ball drop with my family? No. Am I out clubbing with a bunch of my friends? Nope. Instead, I'm sitting here watching Dick Clark, who I hate, eating Cool Ranch Doritos, and waiting for the stupid ball to drop so I can go to bed.

What puts someone like myself in this situation? Simple: I am not a lucky guy. Supposedly I was going to spend this festive holiday with my parents and their friends. Unfortunately, for me that is, I wasn't actually invited. When did I find out about this you ask? 2:48PM, December 31st. Great.

"Well gosh," you're thinking, "Why doesn't he ring in the new year with his girlfriend? They can have a wonderful new-year's kiss and finally say goodbye under the light of dawn." One problem. No girlfriend. I assure you, I've tried many times to remedy the situation, all to no avail. "Maybe his friends," you think. "He could spend the evening with his friends." That one didn't pan out either. It's surprising how difficult it is to find anyone without plans seven hours before midnight.

Anyway, allow me to introduce myself. My name is William Larkin. I'm seventeen and a junior at Milaca High School. My favorite color is blue, I believe that Elvis is dead, and I have no interest in changing my long distance carrier or purchasing aluminum siding. The rest you'll have to figure out for yourself.

So I sit on the couch, waiting for the evening to end. I look down at the bag of chips lying on the floor nearby. For some reason the Doritos go from being something I rather enjoy to being something I can't stand. I trot downstairs to find something else to snack on. This habit of mine bothers me greatly; whenever I'm home alone it seems like I'm always eating something. If I end up living alone for any period of time I'll probably weigh 400lbs and have to travel around by forklift.

I pad into the kitchen and toss the Doritos back into the cabinet. My dog, Shadow, lifts her head to investigate. She's a Springer Spaniel and will turn thirteen this year. She drops her head again and dozes off; apparently I'm not that interesting.

I rifle through the fridge, nudging jars of mayonnaise and strawberry jam aside in hopes of finding something more appetizing. No such luck. I settle for a can of Dr Pepper. I've always wondered where the period at the end of Dr went. Maybe it just fell off. I guess the Coca-Cola Company will need to find a new brand of text adhesive.

I pop the tab on the can of soda and flick on the yard light. It's starting to snow again, leaving a light coat of powder on top of the already white landscape. It's really a beautiful night, even if it is New Year's and I'm stuck at home.

Snow is always pretty in the country. In the cities it gets gritty and black from all the road salt, exhaust, and hobos that pollute it. Out here though, the snow stays clean, pure.

Our land includes 40 acres of swamp and woodland outside of Milaca, Minnesota. I know the area well, it was my stomping grounds up until about the time I was twelve and found out about girls.

Milaca isn't my favorite place to be, but isn't horrible either. It's just a tad bit small. Within the city limits there are twelve churches, two bars, and one stoplight. The largest business in town is the grocery store, and the largest institution is the public school. I swear, the streets are dead after 8PM.

I turn off the yard light and head back upstairs. It's 11:52, almost time for them to drop the ball. Well, I guess it's actually time for the ball to drop again; we're two hours behind Eastern Time so it's already 1:52 there. The partygoers are well on their way to getting hammered in New York.

Finally the ball drops. I don't feel satisfied or fulfilled, I just feel tired. I wander back to the kitchen and throw my can in the recycling. I want to be in bed by the time my parents get home so I don't have to talk to them. It's nothing personal, I'm just feeling fairly depressed and I really don't want to talk to anyone at the moment.

I turn off the kitchen light and slip on a pair of boots. I snatch my father's wool coat from the rack by the door.

"Shadow, come here." She doesn't listen. She doesn't even lift her head. The past six months or so she's either been going deaf or she's starting to ignore me. I wave my arms around, eventually getting her attention. I turn toward the door and she picks herself up and follows, her toenails clicking across the kitchen floor. I hold the door for Shadow and then we step into the cold night.

The snowfall has picked up and my footsteps creak as I walk to the garage. I pour fresh food into her bowl and close the latch to her kennel. I take another look around, taking in the winter scenery. I let out a sigh, breathing a stream of vapor out in front of me. What a lousy way to spend New Year's.

CHAPTER 2

I spend my last day of Christmas Vacation doing nothing constructive whatsoever. My day doesn't start until 11AM, and most
of it is spent surfing the net, playing computer games, and reading
back issues of Bicycling Magazine. Afterward I head straight to bed.
Not a bad day by any measure, but not great either.

The alarm tears me rudely from my sleep. I flail around blindly,
hoping to slap the snooze button. Ah, success. The offending alarm
is defeated. It's always nice to start the day with a victory of some
sort. Maybe the rest of my morning will follow suit. I spend the next
nine minutes drifting in and out of sleep, trying to plan my day and
grab a few more minutes of shut-eye at the same time. I end up being
only moderately successful at both.

It should be a routine day; the only thing I have to remember is
that we have play practice after school. The alarm goes off again, and
I snap it off as I swing myself out of bed. My bed itself is lofted to a
height of four feet to accommodate the ever-growing amount of
stuff in my room. I hop out bed and land in the only clear space on
my floor. I clear the same space every night before I go to bed for this
exact purpose. I'll never forget the time I landed on my stainless steel
coffee mug and almost broke my foot. I crouch as I land to avoid the

shock to my ankles. Before I learned this little trick I would usually greet each new day with stinging feet.

Before getting dressed I shower, shave, put in my contacts, and brush my teeth. When done I strap on my watch (which was formerly my father's), load my pockets (2 pens, 1 pencil, and my wallet), and apply a touch of cologne (Adventurer by Eddie Bauer), then grab my backpack and head upstairs. My father is also getting ready to leave.

"You going to be home tonight?" he asks. I fill up my coffee mug and poke through the fridge, looking for some cream.

"Yeah, I'll be home after practice. Did Mom use all the cream?"

"Yep, you'll have to use milk."

"Pity," I say, grabbing the skim milk.

"When do you work this week?" he asks, shuffling papers into his briefcase. He's referring to my job as a waiter at a local Embers. It's not extravagant work, but it pays.

"I don't,"

"Why not?"

"With play practice I can't work 'till 5:30, so it's hard to get me scheduled."

I end up using the milk in my coffee, which is too bad. Using milk cools down the coffee too fast and doesn't add as much flavor. It's a small, petty point, but it's still worth mentioning.

"See you tonight," I say. I grab my jacket, shoulder my backpack, and head for the door. Outside it's warmed up some, and the windows of my car are completely frosted up. My ride is a 1986 Oldsmobile Calais. I got it from my parents for my sixteenth birthday; they picked it up from my uncle for about $1000. He in turn got it from his used car lot. Apparently the owner was some old lady who wintered in Texas. The car was driven only in the summer, and as a result it's in nice condition and has about 70,000 miles on it. I can't drag race the Olds, but it gets me to school all right.

When I get to school I fall in line to eat breakfast. Up until this year I've eaten breakfast at home, but now I've been eating at school. The selection is much better, to say nothing of the company (my parents aren't very chipper in the morning).

I select the usual for breakfast: a caramel roll, a bowl of Lucky Charms, apple juice, and skim milk. Today the caramel roll is a bit of a risk, it's the first day of school for the week and they might be cold, but I'm willing to gamble.

I sit in the same place I do nearly every morning: northeast table, second seat from the end on the left side. The lunchroom is fairly empty; none of my friends have arrived yet so I eat alone. The caramel roll ends up being surprisingly warm; it must have been made sometime this morning. Just as I'm finishing up Aaron arrives.

Aaron is a freshman, short for his age, with pale blond hair. I met him in marching band, but I didn't really notice him for a while. I started paying attention to him when he dropped Carla Henley's gerbil into her saxophone. We've been friends ever since.

"Hey Will."

"Good morning," I say. "Good vacation?"

"Not bad."

"Anything interesting happen?"

He grins. "Nothing besides the live chicken bowling." This gets my attention.

"Chicken bowling? What did you do now?" I ask.

"Remember when I told you I was going to my grandpa's farm for Christmas?" he says.

"Yeah."

"Well, after brunch on Christmas Day my cousins and I were out looking for something to do, and we wandered into the chicken barn."

"Aaron, what did you do wrong?" I ask, suspecting the worst.

"We bowled," he says, grinning.

"What do you mean 'we bowled'?"

"We set up some milk cartons as pins, tied a chicken into a ball and bowled."

I laugh. I can't help it. "What on earth possessed you to bowl with a live chicken?"

"Dunno, but it seemed like a good idea at the time."

"When did it turn into a not so good idea?" I ask.

"When the chicken died."

"It died?!"

"Yeah, we buried it in the snow behind the barn. I hope the dogs find it before my uncle does." He shrugs, sheepishly.

"Wow, my vacation sounds boring compared to yours."

"Why, what did you do?"

"Nothing. It was boring."

"Did you hear about Adam's sister?" Aaron asks.

"You mean Melinda? No, what happened?" You see, Melinda is my friend Adam's older sister. She's also incredibly attractive, a fact that we never let Adam forget.

"She's going post-secondary next semester," he says.

My jaw drops.

"Wait. That means she'll attend classes at college, she won't even be here!" This takes a moment to sink in. "Who are we going to stare at during study hall?"

"Beats me, I just found out this morning," he says.

I see Adam before third hour. He's short, stubborn, and muscular from his years of wrestling. He's also fairly quiet, unless he's among friends.

"Whaddya <u>mean</u> she's going PSEO!?" I yell, throwing my hands up in the air.

"Good morning to you too," he says.

"Well now who am I going to gawk at?" He's heard this kind of thing before; it doesn't seem to bother him much.

"How'd you hear about it?" he asks.

"Aaron told me. How could you?"

"How could I what?"

"How could you let her go?" I yell.

He smiles. "I <u>told</u> her to go."

"Why in the world would you do that?" I ask.

"That way I can keep her away from you freaks," he says, his smile widening. I turn away in mock anger, trying my best not to laugh.

I even see Sara between in the halls classes, but we don't get a chance to talk. I've been attracted to Sara Fuller since last August. Today she's dressed in jeans and a Dave Matthew's Band shirt; she looks wonderful. Her shoulder-length hair looks different than it did before winter break, but I don't want to say anything about it. I don't want to look stupid if she didn't get it cut. Her hair is brown, lighter than my own, and flows lightly about her face. I'm not sure if she knows how much I care about her, even though I've wanted to tell for such a long time. I haven't, at least not yet. On the other side of the coin, I have no idea how she feels about me. I'm not sure if she'd date me or not. It's strange, I usually don't have any problem talking to people, but I get nervous whenever I talk to her. Stupid hormones.

My morning classes end up being fairly tough, well, besides band. All of the teachers seem to think that because we've had a break they should pile on the homework to make up for lost time. Study hall doesn't come soon enough. I never use my study hall for these stacks of homework, but it does let me relax a little.

You see, my schedule worked out quite well this year. During fourth hour I go to 25 minutes of study hall, then to lunch for a half hour, then back to study hall for another 25 minutes. It works out to be a much-appreciated mid-day break. On top of that, Scott, Adam, and Paul are all in the same study hall. Every day we play hearts. We keep a detailed win/loss record, and things can get quite competitive. If someone is gone one day Mr. Brands plays for them, but if two of us are gone play is suspended for a day. Mr. Brands is our study hall supervisor, and he's not a bad card player either.

Scot Lane is my best friend; he has been since elementary school. We tell each other everything. Well, for the most part. There was the time when he kissed a girl and didn't tell me for four months. Four months! I was furious. Anyway, Scott is a runner. He looks like one too, tall and lanky. He's never had a girlfriend, but the guy never hesitates to help me with my love life, or lack thereof. He's a good advisor though; he tends to keep me from going off the deep end.

You've met Adam, so the only one left is Paul, our fourth player. Paul Hackenhausen may very well be the most stubborn person I know. A small, religious kid, he has his opinions and clings to them like a drowning man clings to a life vest in a hurricane. He's interesting though, and you can't play hearts with three people.

I slide into my seat as the bell rings. Paul is already dealing, and Scott digs out our scorecard from his pile of homework.

"You guys hear about Melinda?" I ask.

Scott looks up from his cards. "No, what happened?"

I glance over to Adam.

"Go ahead," I nod to him, "Tell 'em."

Adam shrugs, "It's not important."

I shake my head and say, "The hell it's not important, tell the poor man."

Adam turns to Scott, "She's taking her classes at the community college next year."

Scott almost drops his cards.

"Didn't she consider our feelings?" he asks.

"Apparently not," I reply.

Paul plays a card, starting the game.

"What's the big deal about that?" he asks.

I shoot a glance at him.

"Unless you haven't noticed, not all of us have a girlfriend hanging on our arms," I say.

"She's not my girlfriend." Paul fidgets a bit.

"Wait a minute," Scott says, "Amy, the girl who hangs on you all of the time, the girl that you meet at the movies every Friday, she's not your girlfriend?"

Paul shakes his head, "Nope."

"Then what is she?" I ask.

Paul shrugs, "Well, she can't date until she's eighteen."

"What exactly are you doing then?" says Scott.

Paul thinks for a moment before he replies. "Whatever you call being as close to dating as you can be…without dating."

Scott smiles, "Sounds like dating to me."

I decide to mess with Paul, just a little bit.

"So Paul," I say, "you get to third base with her yet?"

Amy is the daughter of Paul's pastor; her parents keep her on a pretty short leash. Nevertheless, this comment annoys Paul to no end.

"N-no!" he sputters.

Adam catches on, "Aw, come on," he says, "you've been slammin' the preacher's daughter, haven't you?"

By now Paul's almost yelling, "Of course not!" he says.

"Paul, Paul, Paul," I say, shaking my head. "Taking advantage of poor Amy like that. I have never been so ashamed of you."

CHAPTER 3

So things go, through lunch and study hall. I trudge through three more classes before I'm finally released on my own accord. I manage to find Scott before he goes running.

"Hey Scott, have you seen Sara?"

"No, why?"

"Damn, I wanted to talk to her before she leaves."

He shakes his head, "Sorry, can't help ya." Then he slams his locker shut and walks with me down the hallway.

"Have the odds changed with her at all?" he asks.

I think a minute before answering, "Well, I didn't see her at all over break, so it's been quite awhile. I'd say they've dropped to around forty three percent."

"Forty three percent overall, or within a period of time?" he asks.

"Overall, I'm not about to set a time limit."

"All right," he says, "Well, I'll see you later." He turns into the next hallway and is lost in the crowd.

Scott and I have been calculating odds since our freshmen year. We always try to estimate the probability of a given event. Usually they concern girls, like the odds that Sara will go out with me. We can use it for other things too, like the odds of getting away with some sort of prank. Sure, it's a little juvenile, but it's still fun.

I show up for one act practice early; hopefully I can sneak in a nap before we start. In one act play competition we prepare a one-act play with a cast of less than fifteen actors which runs for less than thirty-five minutes. We then take the play on the road and compete against other schools. Hopefully we make it to the state competition. I've made many friends through one act, and it's been a lot of fun. Truth be told, I've also made some enemies. You can only be around some people for so long before you can't stand them anymore.

Only Bish is in the dim theater when I enter, seated in the audience seating. He's reading a book, <u>The art of Zen Buddhism as Examined by Audrey French</u>. Nathan Bishop may be the most interesting person I know. He's a big guy, about six feet tall, and he must weigh over 230. He always wears a long, gray trench coat and carries a small leather notebook in one pocket. He looks up from his book as the door closes behind me.

"Salutations William."

"Hi Bish, how's the book?"

I sit on the back of a seat two rows in front of him, letting my bag drop into the seat next to me.

"It's excellent," he says, "It inspects Zen Buddhism as a philosophy rather then as a religion. It's quite insightful really."

"Sounds great," I mutter.

"Young Julian was searching for you earlier," Bish says, raising his eyebrows slightly. "She seemed quite eager to see you."

I sigh "Wonderful. I can't find Sara, but Julie is probably hunting me as we speak."

Julie Morgan has a crush on me; she has for the past month or so. I can only hope that it passes soon so I can quit looking over my shoulder. I hate it when I feel like prey.

"How are things going with Sweet Sara?" Bish asks.

I would usually smack someone fore calling her Sweet Sara, but I let it go. It's as close as he ever gets to a compliment.

"Not too bad. Odds are at forty three percent."

His brow furrows, "A slight slip from before break, isn't it?"

I nod, "I didn't see her at all over vacation."

"A delay of game penalty, so to speak," Bish says, smiling.

I laugh, "Yeah, so to speak."

The door opens behind me and I turn around, hoping that it's not Julie. Luckily, it's Allison. She trudges in, hurls her bag into one of the seats, and stomps backstage. If she's in a bad mood she usually heads to the couch in the storeroom to sulk. I get up to follow her.

Al Kelly is another, well, eccentric individual. She's a full-fledged vegetarian, hasn't eaten meat since eighth grade. Al would like to think of herself as a human rights activist, and she could make a great feminist if she put her mind to it. She's also one of my closest friends.

I walk backstage, weave my way through the curtains, and sit next to her on the "sex couch," as it's commonly called. The couch sits in a small alcove, nearly surrounded by pieces of furniture and platforms used by previous plays.

"Bad day?" I ask, hoping I don't piss her off even more. She can be volatile if she wants to.

"Nope," she says, "it was just wonderful."

"What happened?" I ask.

"I hate men."

I cringe, "Ouch."

"Not you," she says, "it's Griffin."

I frown a bit and say, "Griffin like your ex-boyfriend Griffin?"

"The same," she says, her shoulders slumping.

Allison dated Griffin for four and a half months, 138 days to be exact. She devoted herself to him, but he was always distant, busy with other things. He always managed to push her away. Jerk. They finally broke up about six months ago. She took it pretty hard.

"What did he do now?" I ask.

She sighs, "He walked by me in the hallway."

"Uh, I'm afraid I don't follow," I say, not really understanding.

She slides down in her seat. "Why can't he just date me again?"

"Al, not this again. I thought you said you were over him."

She looks down, fidgeting with the ring on her thumb.

"Yeah, me too."

"Listen to me," I say, "you can do <u>better</u> than him." I hate it when she's like this.

She looks up at me, "Yeah, I guess. Why do most guys have to be such jerks?"

I shake my head. "You've got me. That's why I hang out with you." She gives a little smile. I hear the door to the theater open and voices enter from the hall. I take her hand. "Come on," I say, pulling her up, "let's go put on a play."

Play practice goes well, we only run through the performance once. Our director, Samuel "Mad Jack" Jackson, when he's mad, can be unbearable. This afternoon he's in good spirits though, joking with the cast and letting small mistakes go by without criticism.

Afterwards, Richard helps me with my chemistry. Richard Harris and I have been friends since grade school. He's tall and thin with wire rimmed glasses and black hair. The guy's a math wizard, and he hates jocks with a passion. He also prides himself in being a non-conformist.

"So we can't change the subscripts on the equations?" I ask.

"No," he says, "just the coefficients."

I hate balancing equations. I jot down a few notes and flip my notebook shut.

"I'm down to forty three percent," I say.

"What?"

I explain. "With Sara, overall, I'm down to forty three percent."

"I don't get it," he says.

I let out a sigh. I hate having to explain this very often.

"All things considered, I have a forty three percent chance of dating Sara."

He shakes his head. "That's stupid."

"What?!" I say, "How can that be stupid?"

"You can't be close to accurate, there are too many variables," he replies.

"I figure that the odds are accurate within five or ten percent," I explain.

"Why do you have to give the percent anyway?" he asks, "Why don't you just say that the odds are worse?"

I smile, "It's more fun this way."

He shakes his head again. Sometimes I think having fun is a foreign concept to Richard. Now and then he just doesn't seem to understand it. That poor kid.

CHAPTER 4

One more hour. That's all, one more brief, minuscule hour. I've only been back to school two days and already Ms. Boyer is sending me into a coma. She stands at the front of the room, a tall woman in a business suit with short black hair. She talks about something grammar-ish; prepositions, I think. I haven't really listened for the past five or ten minutes.

In all fairness, I've been against Ms. Boyer from the start. She talks to a class of juniors like we're in second grade. On top of that she has bad grammar. She's and ENGLISH teacher for Chrissake! They should have a screening process for that sort of thing. I glance up at the clock, 47 minutes left.

"Will, would you care to add to David's comment?" Ms. Boyer's voice slices into my thought process. I look around; everyone is looking at me, expecting me to say something.

"Uh, no, that about sums it up," I say, hoping she'll leave me alone. Boyer just shoots me an evil glance. I think the glance is saying "PAY ATTENTION!" She may have thrown in some expletives too; I'm not very good at reading glances. Maybe they offer a class for it somewhere.

I look over at Dave, who must have had a hand in the ordeal. He grins smugly. God I hate him.

Wait, allow me to elaborate, I hate him a lot. I really hate him. I hate him with all of my being. I'll explain. I was in sixth grade and playing summer baseball. I was playing at second base, as was David Williams. He didn't really like me, I didn't really like him. Things went downhill from there. Our rivalry lasted for years, ending in the summer of ninth grade when I finally quit after the season was over. Right now he's the starting second baseman on our varsity team. After awhile I cooled down a bit and figured that he may be an all right guy. Then I found out that he likes Sara. I hated him then, and now I can't stand the kid.

He goes through girlfriends like water, and he always makes sure to slobber on them in the halls for everyone to see. He is prince charming when he's around women, but when they leave he's prince jackass. He even listens to rap. This doesn't necessarily make him a bad person, but I hate rap. On top of everything, the prick is also in my seventh hour English class. What a way to end the day.

I look at the clock again, 38 minutes to go. Our English Department must be working for the government; they've found a way to slow down time. Uh oh, everyone is taking out their English Lit. books, I guess I should do the same.

The next 38 minutes go by fairly painlessly, I only slip out of consciousness once or twice. The real agony arrives when Julie finds me in the hall. I've been trying to dodge her for the past week, and I guess she's catching on.

"Hey Will!" she says, hugging me from behind. Julie is fairly short, with long blond hair. She wants desperately to be popular, but she's only moderately successful. She's also not my type.

"Hello Julie," I say, shrugging her off.

"Did you have a good day?" she asks, smiling sweetly.

"Getting worse," I mumble. Usually I'm nice to her, but I'm in no mood to deal with this now.

"Aww," she says, frowning, "What's wrong? Is Willie down in the dumps?"

"Hey Julie," I say, looking over her shoulder, "Isn't that your dad?"

"What?!"

She turns around, I bolt. Hopefully I can avoid her until tomorrow. I'm in a hurry today though, I have to work at 3:30 and it's 3:10 now. If the traffic out of the school parking lot isn't too bad I can still make it.

I work as a waiter at the Embers in town. The job isn't bad; I make enough on tips to get me through the week. That allows me to place all of my paychecks into savings; a fairly convenient way to save money. I guess my biggest complaint isn't the customers, it's the staff. Lisa, our manager, may have one of the coldest hearts in the world. I swear, ice water must flow through her veins. I am the only waiter, and the rest of the wait staff is made up of cranky women who are always in a bad mood and usually on break.

Miraculously, I make it to work in time. I end up punching in at 3:28; not just on time, but early. I toss my jacket and backpack into the dark, smoky break room. Mary sits at the table, playing solitaire and taking a drag on her cancer sticks. My parents wonder why my jacket smells like cigarettes every night.

Surprisingly, it turns out to be a relatively busy evening. I end up serving three separate groups of snowmobilers, all of which tip generously. I like them, tipping well is an easy way to make new friends. It's a fairly good night, and our manager only yells at me once.

"Guess who I just got done talking to," Lisa says.

I drop the dirty plates I'm carrying into the dish cart and sigh. Then I ask, "Was it Willie Nelson?"

She is not amused. "No. It was not Willie Nelson. I just talked to the man who was sitting in table thirty, and he was pretty damn upset at you."

"It shows," I say, "he gave me a fifteen cent tip."

Lisa scowls; she would fire me, she reminds me of the fact every night. Luckily Barbara, the owner, likes me.

"He said you gave him pickles with his burger," she says.

"Pickles come with all of the burgers!" I say, rolling my eyes.

"The man is allergic to pickles!" she yells, "He started breaking out in hives!"

Now she's starting to piss me off. I have better things to do than have this conversation. "Listen," I say, "look around. This is a restaurant. Most customers don't provide a medical record. He didn't tell me, I didn't know. I am not about to ask every customer if they are allergic to pickles, so get off my back about it."

I turn and walk away. Most of our arguments end like this, we both end up mad and nothing is accomplished.

At the end of the night I pull of my olive green apron and slide into a booth. I check my watch, it's 9:30. I pull from my apron wads of dollar bills and a fistful of change. All told it's $37.28. Not too bad. I get up and check the schedule; I don't work at all next week. Damn, cash is running short around here. I hardly worked at all over break, and I only work tonight this week and no hours next week. Not a good sign.

I punch out, grab my smoke-infused jacket, and head for the door. I walk across the frigid parking lot until I get to my car, the good old Calais.

I heave my bag into the passenger seat and slide in. It starts easily enough, but I know that it'll stall if I don't let it warm up. I tap the gas and brakes to make sure neither is frozen, and the engine hums politely. Before putting on my gloves I slide in a CD, The Definitive Blues Brothers Collection. I look at the windshield. Even with the defroster cranking out heat the windshield is still covered with ice. Damnit. I grudgingly grab my scraper and get out to start chipping.

CHAPTER 5

$\mathcal{A}$ few more hours and I will be gifted with the sweet, glorious weekend. I toss my backpack next to my study hall seat and pull the closest three desks together, forming an X. Mr. Brands, our study hall teacher and occasional Hearts advisor looks up from his magazine. Brands is tall and lanky, in his twenties. He's easy to get along with, and I've liked him since the beginning of the semester.

"Don't you guys ever work in study hall?" Brands asks.

"No, we don't need to," I say, shuffling the cards. Scott, Adam, and Paul trickle in as I deal. "'Bout time you guys get here."

"Yeah, Paul just HAD to drop his books off at his locker," Scott says.

"They were heavy," Paul adds.

"Maybe for you," Adam replies, sliding into his seat. I finish dealing and we all pick up our hands. I glance at my score sheet to see where we left off.

"Pass left," I say, and the game moves along. Our group has no special attachment to the game of hearts, it just so happens that we all know how to play, and we're all too lazy to learn a new game.

"Geez, why do I always get such crappy hands?" Paul says to no one in particular.

"Quit whining and play," Scott says.

"But this hand sucks." Paul continues, "Why do I always get lousy cards?"

Adam looks up, "Because I love your mom?"

"What?" Paul asks.

"You get lousy cards because I love your mom," Adam says, enjoying himself.

"Shut up," Paul snaps.

"I love your sister too, she's hot," Adam says. Paul's sister is in fourth grade.

"Quit it!"

"Your dad's nice too," Adam snickers.

"Would someone hit him?" Paul asks.

"But I like your sister the best. Tell her to come over tonight," Adam grins.

I start laughing. It's all horribly stupid, but I laugh anyway. Play resumes, and a few cards fall without comment. Then I speak up.

"Would you cut off your own finger for a million dollars?"

A short pause.

"Which finger?" Scott asks.

"Left index," I say, choosing a finger that's significant but not critical.

"With or without anesthesia?" Paul asks.

"Only general anesthesia, but you have to be the one doing the cutting," I reply.

Adam answers first. "I think I would. I could use a million dollars a lot more than this finger."

Paul and Adam both nod.

"All right," I say, "What about this. If time, location, and salary were all of no object, what would be your dream job?"

Apparently this requires some deep inflection, because the group is silent for a minute or two.

"An early Olympic wrestler," Adam says, sitting up in his chair. I guess he's proud of his revelation.

"Why?" I ask.

"Well," he says, "Think about it. You get to throw guys around, prance in front of chicks naked, and then get all the girls."

"You sick bastard," Scott says, disgusted.

"What?"

"You just want to wrestle with naked guys! That's sick."

"Oh yeah, what would you do?" Adam asks.

"I'd be the founder of Microsoft," Scott says.

"Just for the money?" I ask, "You don't need job satisfaction or anything like that?

"Hey, with that much money I can buy satisfaction."

I turn to Paul, "What about you?"

"I would be Peter the Apostle," he says.

I roll my eyes, "You are such a dork."

"Think about it, there's nothing better than an eternity in heaven."

I hate it when he gets theological. Gives me the creeps.

"I couldn't be an apostle; too much walking," I say.

"What would you be then?" he asks.

"Napoleon. I'd get to conquer most of Europe, be feared by my enemies, and order people around," I say. I also happen to know that Napoleon supposedly only had one testicle, but I don't tell them that.

"Hmm, not bad," Scott says, considering the perks of being the leader of a great army, "But it sounds fairly stressful. I still want to run Microsoft.

I glance at my watch, "I'd still like to eat lunch," I say, getting out of my desk. We wave to Mr. Brands and head out, reaching the lunchroom thirty seconds before the bell rings. I look at our menu for the day: Breaded Chicken Patty or Pork Steak on a Bun. I opt for a salad and some soup, a tasty chicken noodle. I try to avoid meals that include compressed meat parts. I've cut into those chicken patties before and I think I saw a vein once.

The four of us sit at a small round table in the center of the lunch-room. Along with the card players sit Richard and Aaron. Pete Roden, a ninth grader and a close friend of Aaron, usually joins us every other day. He's on a block schedule so he doesn't eat the same lunch all the time. Today is his off day, so we'll see him tomorrow. It's just the six of us, Paul with his bag lunch and the rest of us with our cafeteria gruel.

"I heard we get to see a liquid nitrogen experiment in chemistry," Richard says, picking at his pork steak.

"Nope, it's postponed until Monday," I reply.

"Man, liquid nitrogen is cool, we should get some," Scott says, working around a mouthful of salad.

I vaguely remember a demonstration in seventh grade where we froze a racquetball and shattered it. It was pretty cool.

"We could freeze all kinds of stuff," Scott continues.

"Hey, do you think we could revive things?" Richard asks, looking up from his tray.

"What do you mean?" I ask.

"Like, could we freeze a rat and then revive it?"

"No way," Paul says, "The freezing would kill it."

"You sure?" Richard asks, "It might work." He seems quite attached to the idea. He looks to me for support.

"Well," I say, "How does frostbite work?"

"The cells freeze," he says, "The water within them explodes and the cells die."

I think about this for a bit, slurping down soup.

"Wouldn't most of the mouse's cells explode? I don't think he'd do very well if we unfroze him," I say. All I can picture is the little mouse reduced to a puddle of fur and bones after his cells explode. Not a pretty sight.

CHAPTER 6

Not once. Not once has Barbara ever called me at home. I stand in my kitchen, listening to her ask me about my schedule requests. What is she doing calling on a Saturday? She doesn't sound the same either, she sounds tense somehow. At first I thought she wanted me to work today, but she only talks about the schedule.

"I'm sorry Barb," I say, "But play practice runs every night until five or five thirty, and I'm usually busy on the weekends. I'll be free when the play is over."

Then I figure it out. She begins talking about the problems she's had balancing the schedule, and I finally catch on. I am about to be fired. She keeps talking, but I don't really hear it. Only pieces of what she says gets through, "Good waiter, slow winter, too many on the staff, sorry I have to let you go." I slowly realize that she's finished, and it's my turn to talk. I consider yelling, but I'm not really all that mad. I'm not happy either. I don't really know how I feel.

"I guess I'm sorry it didn't work out," I say, still slightly stunned. It feels like I'm breaking up with her.

She goes on about references and that maybe I can come back in the summer.

"Is that it?" I ask.

"Yes, I'll send you your last paycheck in the mail."

"Well, goodbye then," I say, and it's over.

I hang up without waiting for her reply. I stand there for a minute, staring blankly at the phone. I was just fired. The concept still seems foreign. I take a quick inventory of my assets. I've got about $200 in checking and $1,000-$1,500 in savings. I don't want to hit up my savings account if I don't have to, but I'd rather do that than go begging to my parents. I sigh. A job hunting I will go, a job hunting I will go, hi ho the derry-o…

I walk over to the couch and fall onto it. I stare up at the ceiling of our A-frame house fifteen feet over my head. Where else can I work around here? I'm not going to end up bagging groceries and making minimum wage, I'd go crazy. I don't want to work at Parson's Manufacturing either. I couldn't work on an assembly line. I think that would push me over the edge; I'd go psycho and spend my days twitching in a corner and mumbling incoherently. There are a few other restaurants in town; I guess I'll start with them.

"What's wrong with you?"

I turn around to see my father standing behind me.

"Dad, do you know how to put together a resume?"

"Sure, is it for an English project or something?"

"Nope, it's for getting a job."

He pauses for a moment, "What do you mean?"

"That was Brenda on the phone, I'm officially fired."

His face hovers between sympathy and accusation. When he's standing he's not much taller than me, but as I sit on the couch he seems huge.

"What did you do?" he asks, choosing his words carefully.

"Nothing, that's the problem."

His brow furrows. He runs his hand across his head, a habit that may or may not be the cause of his receding hairline. I decide to elaborate.

"It was a scheduling conflict, the play screwed things up and I couldn't work often enough."

Dad relaxes a little, and he shrugs slightly, "So now what?" he asks.

I'm pretty sure that a correct answer to this question is critical. "Well," I say, "I'm going to pick up applications from some restaurants in town on Monday, put together a resume, and start with that."

"Are you sure you want to work during school?"

"What?" I ask. The question catches me off guard. He's the one who wanted me to get a job in the first place.

"Instead of working now, you could just work in the summer," he says.

"Doing what?"

"You could work construction. Ten to fifteen dollars an hour, five days a week."

I can see where this is going, and I don't like the sound of it.

"I'd much rather be a waiter," I say, hoping to settle the issue.

"You'd rather work nights like you have been?"

"Yes, I want my summer to be a vacation. I like the hours I work," I say in my defense. I hate it when I'm defending myself; it feels like I'm always retreating.

"All right," he says, crossing his arms, "If that's what you want." This settled, he turns and heads upstairs. I hear the TV click on…basketball.

Ugh, I have to get a job. Well, maybe it won't be so bad. The manager might actually be nice. Maybe, if I'm lucky, the other employees will actually do some work. I should be careful though, don't want to get too optimistic.

CHAPTER 7

*L*ater that day I retire to my room and slump into my beanbag chair to survey the situation. I have a partial resume from last year; I made a short one for the job at Embers. All that's left to decide is where to apply.

I guess my first option is Ray's. The place serves the best fried chicken in town. More importantly, most of the waitresses are extremely attractive. Talk about fringe benefits.

Then there's the Pizza Hut in town. I guess the work wouldn't be bad, but I've heard that the manager's a head case. I've been through enough of that already. I don't enjoy working for wackos.

Let's see, the only other restaurant in town is the Sportsman's Cafe. From what I remember it's the gathering place for the elderly people in town. I guess it's the big hangout for the over sixty-five crowd.

I sit up and look around my room. My beanbag sits exactly in the center, surrounded by clothes of varying levels of cleanliness. Piles of clean clothes sit on top of my dresser, but I'm not going to put them away. I'll probably wear them before that, and it's easier to find what I want when everything is in it's own pile instead of in a drawer.

My eyes shift to my bookshelves, most of the space filled with paperbacks. I walk over to the corner bookcase and kneel down to the bottom shelf. It is here where I keep some of the most important parts of my life. In the shelf lie three stuffed scrapbooks, a pile of file folders, and one manila pouch. I pull out the pouch and open it. Inside are a hundred or so folded pieces of notebook paper and a few assorted letters. I dump the entire contents of the envelope onto the floor. In front of me is every important note, letter, or e-mail I have received from any girl in the past four or five years. I sigh, chose a note at random, and open it.

Ah yes, Jamie Salstrom, my first actual girlfriend. We were together at the end of eighth grade, and the entire relationship ended up lasting about three weeks. She was a thin little girl back then, with big thick glasses. We held hands a lot, but we never kissed. I don't remember much else, except for our night at the movies. My father actually sat behind us. Not much fun at all. I eventually broke up with her; she was beginning to annoy me. Later I also found out that she was cheating on me too. To his credit, Scott did advise against the whole thing. I should have listened to him. She's still in school, but I haven't talked to her in a year or two. She could fall off the face of the earth and it wouldn't affect my life much one way or the other. Let's try another letter.

Amber Marudas, the second of my official relationships. We dated for two months during the beginning of this past year. She's home schooled, a friend of Paul's. I met her at a basketball game and she caught my attention. She was attractive, fairly interesting, and she carried herself well. After that Paul was my informant, telling me what she was up to and what she was telling her friends about me. We went out on four or five dates, nothing very spectacular. When I was dating her I still liked Sara, and Amber didn't seem to intent on moving our relationship along very fast, so things stayed fairly casual. It was odd, the whole relationship didn't carry much weight for me, and I wasn't that attached to her. It was like having another hobby. I was nice to have someone there for me though. Eventually, things fell apart.

You see, the girl didn't talk. For the most part we just plain didn't have conversations. I talked. She listened. That was about it. In my defense, I tried to work things out. I would ask questions, give her opportunities to talk. It was no use; maybe I just talk too much. Honestly though, she didn't really have an opinion on anything; at least not that I could find. She just agreed to everything. I have more opinions than I know what to do with. I guess it just wasn't meant to be. I fold the letter and toss it back onto the pile.

My eyes wander back up to my alarm clock. It's 6:58PM, time to check out the TV movies for the evening. As I walk out of my room I realize the significance of those thoughts. I know the Saturday night TV schedule. In it's own special way, that fact is very, very sad. I need to get a life.

CHAPTER 8

❀

*I*t's strange; days off of school are so much better than plain old weekends. Colors are brighter, the air is sweeter, and food tastes better. I love Martin Luther King; he was kind enough to give us the day off.

It's 1PM and I drive along in my Olds, heading toward Scott's house. Our plan is to go into St. Cloud for the day instead of sitting on our asses at home. St. Cloud is the closest city of respectable size, and we go there quite a bit. It's ten times the size of Milaca, giving it a population of about 40,000. Division Street, the four-lane road that cuts right through the heart of the city, dominates the city. It's possible to hit almost every mall and major retailer in St. Cloud and never get off Division.

Our excursions to St. Cloud rarely have a set purpose. Now and then we'll be looking for something in particular, but we usually go for the sake of going. Today we were talking about seeing a movie, but I doubt that we'll actually do it. Although we'll never admit it, it's a little pathetic to go to a film without any ladies along with us.

I pull into his driveway five minutes early. I almost get out of the car to get him, but then I see him shuffling around near the door. He trots out to the car, wearing his Columbia jacket and a ridiculous looking stocking hat. The hat is striped with bold lines of red, white, and orange and is topped off with a little fluffy ball. He opens the passenger side door and almost gets in when I hold up my hand to stop him.

"You're not getting into my car like that," I say, holding my hand in front of him.

"Why not?" he asks.

"You've gotta take that hat off first," I say, pointing at his head.

He looks up, "What's wrong with my hat?"

"It's horribly ugly," I reply, "Nothing that grotesque can ride in my car." He still doesn't look convinced. "On top of that, as your best friend I can't allow you to commit a fashion sin such as this. I'm doing you a favor."

He finally rolls his eyes and gives up, pulling off his hat and sliding into the car. I shove the vehicle into drive and we pull away from the house.

"When did you wake up?" I ask. He was asleep when I called him in the morning. Lazy bum.

He glances at his watch, "'Bout an hour ago."

"Did you hear the big news yet?" I ask.

"No, what?"

"You are looking at an unemployed man," I say, thrusting my chin into the air.

"Really?" he says, his eyes widening, "What happened?"

"Brenda called, talked at me for a bit, and basically said clean out your desk. I guess I couldn't work enough hours, so they canned me."

"Wow," he says, "You're the first person I know that's been fired."

I shrug, "It's not a huge deal."

"Yeah, why not?"

"Well," I think for a minute, "My manager was a bitch, and everyone there was lazy, maybe now I can work with people who, you know, work."

"I suppose," he says, "Think you'll get another job?"

"I sure hope so."

We talk through the rest of the drive, discussing where we're going and what we want to buy. Eventually we agree on the mall as a starting point, and then we'll work our way through the town from there. I'm able to jockey my way through traffic and I finally find a parking space a couple hundred yards from the entrance. I hop out of the car, locking the door behind me. Scott looks over at the entrance.

"Hey, couldn't we park any farther away?" he asks.

"Well," I say, "I wanted to give you a workout, but if you have to walk any farther than this it might kill you."

He smiles, "Yep, I guess we wouldn't want that."

As we walk through the doors, I begin searching. I try to never pass up the chance to find the next Ms. Larkin. Unfortunately all of the girls in sight were either hit with the ugly stick or obviously attached. We snake our way through the crowded mall, starting from the south entrance and working counterclockwise, the same way we always do. Our first stop is Walden Books. I start browsing the magazine rack, my eyes roving over the titles and headlines. Hmm, a photo essay of Alyissa Milano, interesting. I look to my left in time to see a girl, sixteen or so, standing a few feet away. Let's see, if I pick up the magazine the chic might think I'm a pig. Alyissa Milano is pretty hot though. I look at the girl again. She's tall, dark haired, not at all unattractive. I take a deep breath. Let's go for the girl.

I take a few steps closer; she seems to be looking at the photography or art magazines. I pick up Photography Monthly and flip through it. She looks up at me, to both my elation and my horror.

"Are you a photographer?" she asks, her blue eyes shining.

My mind reels, think fast…think fast. Seriously, there is only one answer.

"Why yes I am," I say, "You?"

"I want to be," she replies, "I'm just getting started."

OK, she's a beginner, she doesn't know much. I might be able to pull this off. Come on Will, make some conversation.

"What type of equipment are you starting out with?" I ask.

"I've got a Nikon 350 with a three stage flash and f-stop selector with an 80-200mm lens," she says, "What do you have?"

Oh damn.

"Uh, I've got a Cannon Thirty Five Thousand X." Please God…Please God…

She looks puzzled, "Huh," she says, "I've never seen one of those before. What's it like?"

Time for some quick thinking.

"Well, it's, uh, black. It's got an external flash and a digital light meter readout. Then I also got the 752 telemetrex lens for it too," I say, hoping to sound slightly competent.

"A telemetrex lens?" she says, arching her eyebrows.

Damnit, she must be on to me. Come on Will, figure this out.

"Yeah, it's new this year," I say. She smiles, my line worked!

"Huh, what else did they add this year?" she asks, looking interested.

"Umm, now it runs only on 800-max film and uh, it's digital too," I say, hoping it makes sense.

"Really?"

"Yep, with one thousand megs of, uh, RAM and a hundred million mega pixel clarity. And, ah, it stores four hundred pictures too," I say, forcing a smile.

Then I feel a hand on my shoulder.

"Excuse me miss, is this young man bothering you?"

I turn around and there's Scott.

"I'm sorry about that, Miss. Willie," he says, turning me away from her, "It's time for you to take your medicine now."

Once we turn around the corner I punch him in the arm.

"What the hell did you do that for?!" I hiss, trying to keep my voice down. He just laughs.

"Are you kidding me?" he says, "I saved your sorry ass."

"What? I could have gotten her number!"

He scoffs, "I heard you talking to her, you were making a fool of yourself. A telemeterex lens? Come on."

"OK fine," I say, "Maybe things weren't going perfectly, but I could have pulled it off."

He just shakes his head and starts walking farther into the mall.

I yell at him, "Hey, I could have, I swear! Scott? Hey, wait up!" I run after him.

Our next stop is Sam Goody, the music store. We're not really looking for anything, but it's always interesting to see what we can find. We wander between the racks, flipping through the discs as we go.

"Hey Will, who is Marvin Gaye?" Scott asks, poking his head over the rack between us.

"Hmm, Marvin Gaye…" I think for a moment. Then it clicks, "Oh yeah, Motown, R&B singer, pretty good actually. He sings Let's Get it On, Sexual Healing, a few others. Why?"

Scott looks down, "Because you can get his CD for six bucks."

"Really?" I say, "Lemme see."

He hands me the CD; sure enough, it's Marvin Gaye Live, only $5.99. I think I'll get it.

Scott moves farther down the rack of discs. Then he says, "All right, what about Blues Traveler, who are they?"

My friend Scott is pretty smart, but music he knows not.

"Modern blues band," I reply, "some of the best harmonica solos of all time. Lead singer is John Popper, big guy, they're pretty good too." Scott just nods and continues flipping through discs.

Later, while walking though the wide hallways of the mall, I notice something that catches my eye. Axel Boser, our choir director, walks out of the Victoria's Secret outlet. Now, I'm sure he's not married, and last I heard he didn't have a girlfriend. What could he be doing in there? Puzzling.

The real excitement of the evening occurs across the street in Toys R Us. We're browsing the aisles for something to entertain us in chem. class when I find it. It sits on the shelf in its shining glory: laser tag.

"Pssst, Scott!" I wave him over to me. "Check this out," I say, pointing at the box. His eyes widen. "Well, should we?"

He ponders it for a moment, "Won't we get in trouble?"

I suppose I can't deny it. "We might," I say, letting it hang for a second. "But how often do you come into this place anyway?"

"Well," he says, "I guess the worst thing they can do is kick us out." He smiles.

It ends up to be a very good game, spread over 15 minutes and 14 aisles. A few customers get riled up, to say nothing of the employees, but we have a ball. Oh, and we're also not allowed to go into Toys R Us anymore.

CHAPTER 9

I shoot out of seventh hour English like a rocket, leaping over the bottom five steps of the staircase and almost running over an eighth grader before I get to my locker. Play practice starts in twenty-seven minutes and I have to get two job applications uptown and be back in time. I tear my coat and backpack out of my locker and head for the parking lot. On my way out I swing by Allison's locker.

"Hey Al, wanna go for a ride?" I ask.

She zips up her bag and slams her locker shut, "Sure, where to?"

"I've got to drop off a couple of job applications before practice," I say, as we fight our way through the crowded hallway.

"Don't you work at Embers?" she asks.

"I used to," I say, digging for my keys, "But not anymore." I hate having to explain this to everyone. We burst out of the cafeteria doors and into the sunlight.

"What happened?" she asks.

"The manager's a jerk and I couldn't work enough." I unlock my car and yank open the door, leaving a foot long scratch in the car next to me in the process. I pull the door back but it's too late, a deep gash lies in the shiny red paint.

"Shit!" I yell, upon inspection the gouge. "Whose car is this?"

Allison looks around, checking for witnesses, "It's Luke's, his parents bought it for his birthday, remember?"

I smile; that kid deserves it. I'd nominate him for the moron of the month club if I could. I shrug, slide into my seat, then start the engine.

"So," she says as we pull out of the parking lot, "Is Julie still after you?"

I let out a groan, "Yeah, now worse than ever. Doesn't she get it?"

"Hey," she says, "Look at it this way, at least someone likes you."

"Gee Al, thanks. That really helps."

She smiles, "You know what I mean."

I sigh, "Man, girls are weird. I'll never understand 'em."

She hits my arm with the back of her hand, "No they're not," she says.

"Sure they are. They burn themselves with ultraviolet rays just to look pretty and then plaster their faces with makeup. They don't say how they feel, but then they get mad at us for not understanding them. Face it, girls are just plain weird."

"We're not that bad," she says.

"I suppose they're not completely horrible," I continue, "They do smell better than guys do. They're prettier too."

Our first stop is Ray's. With the establishment's history of attractive waitresses, it's my standout first choice. I throw my car into park and we scramble into the restaurant. As I walk through the door I look around. Megan Larsen is standing at the counter reading the paper. She's tall, with long blond hair, a charming smile, and very large, um, eyes (wink wink). She's the president of the senior class, a state ranked swimmer, and she works at Ray's. Good old fringe benefits.

Allison notices me looking over Megan and punches me in the arm, "Pig," she mutters.

"Hello Megan," I say, smiling brightly.

"Hi," she replies, not even looking up from the newspaper.

"Are you guys accepting job applications?" I ask.

"Probably."

I set my application on the counter, saying "Well, here's mine. I hope you like it." She just nods; either not catching my feeble joke or not appreciating it much. I contemplate trying to continue, but it's useless. She couldn't be more out of my league. I walk out, slightly saddened.

Al, walking behind me, speaks up, "Men are pigs."

"What?" I ask, faking innocence.

"You were totally checking her out," she says, apparently astonished.

"Maybe I glanced once," I reply, opening my car door. "But I wasn't checking her out."

"You were so checking her out!" Al protests, getting into the car, "I can't believe you did that."

I'm surprised this is new to her. "So I check hot girls out, so what? It happens all the time."

"You mean guys do that sort of thing a lot?"

I shrug, "Sure we do, it's part of our nature."

She shakes her head, "Guys are disgusting."

I smile. "Hey, at least we're not weird."

My next and final drop-off is at The Sportsman's Cafe. The smell of cigarette smoke hits me as I walk through the door. Allison cringes too; I guess the smell isn't just my imagination. The place is nearly empty, save an elderly couple in a booth, two guys drinking coffee at the counter, and the waitress. Despite the sunny day the interior is dim, with the scant sunlight filtering through the slight haze of smoke. The only waitress is in her late forties, fairly short, and she hasn't been missing many meals. A far cry from Megan by any measure. There's no need to stare this time.

Altogether the process goes in the same manner, and we're back outside within minutes. We make it back to the school on time, and we walk into the theater just before 3:30.

"If it isn't Sir William and Princess Allison," Bishop declares as we walk in. We're still a little early, and the only other people in the theatre are Bish and Amanda Timmer, our sound techie for the play. Amanda waves and Allison wanders over to talk to her. I walk over to Bish instead, dropping my coat and backpack into one of the seats.

"Bish," I say, "what are you thoughts on Megan Larsen?"

He thinks for a second, then replies, "Well, she's athletic, confident in her abilities, and has a solid work ethic. She depends heavily on others though; not much of an introvert." After a pause he adds, "She also has a very nice rack."

I nod, then ask, "Do you think I have any chance with her?"

"Sir William," he says, "to put it bluntly, no. Even if you did appeal to her by some strange twist of fate, her current boyfriend happens to be bigger, stronger, and faster than you." He pauses for a bit, then he smiles and says, "You are my friend, and I would not want you to spend the rest of your high school career with the nickname 'Hamburger Face.'"

I laugh. He has a point.

"Have you wondered why rabbits aren't more common than they are?" Bish asks, abruptly steering the conversation in a new direction.

"Well," I reply, "I can't say I've given the matter a whole lot of thought. Why?"

"Think about it. They're small, don't eat much, travel quickly and efficiently, and they reproduce in large numbers. In theory, rabbits should rule the world."

I wait a moment for the idea to sink in. "Do you think about these things a lot?" I ask. He doesn't answer me though; he's too deep in thought.

"Maybe," he continues, "Maybe they do rule the earth. We just don't know about it. Maybe they are controlling us and…"

As I walk away Bish trails off. Once again his train of thought is a runaway. When he's like this there's no talking to him, he's off in his own world.

CHAPTER 10

*A*ck, another Thursday night alone. I need to find myself a social life. Hell, I don't even have any homework to do. It seems that my only courses of action are to watch TV or tune my bike for the summer. I end up siding with the latter, not wanting spend any more time in front of the idiot box. I pull on an old hooded sweatshirt and walk out to the garage, flipping on the lights as I enter. Inside sits my father's truck, but not my mother's car. She has a late meeting and won't be home for a couple more hours. Her half of the garage will be my workshop.

Before doing anything else I light the small propane heater to stave off the cold. I roll my bike over to the toolbox and flip the bike upside down to inspect it. I spin the tires to check the hubs, then turn the pedals a few times to make sure the chain hasn't rusted. This done, I begin to dismantle the hubs, starting with the front, so I can repack them with fresh grease. As I begin loosening the outer lock-nuts I contemplate my current position.

As usual, my mind drifts to girls. I really like Sara, and I can hardly stop thinking about her. Then again, I haven't been making a whole lot of progress with her lately. Is it time to start thinking of other options? Well, there's always Julie; but she's not my type, not in the least. I don't think I could date someone who annoys me that much. I would go insane. So she's out of the question. One must not forget about Anna either. Anna Harvey is a distance runner in track in cross-country. She's tall, with long legs and dark brown hair. I've never even had a complete conversation with her, but I'm attracted to her anyway. Seriously, I think it's her eyes. We'll pass each other in the halls, saying nothing, but her eyes talk nonstop. I think they say "Hi Will I really like you marry me and we'll move to the ocean and have lots of kids and a dog or two and we'll be happy forever call me." Or I could be wrong. I guess it really doesn't matter much anyway; she's in eighth grade. Sure, that doesn't mean much to most people, but in this high school it means a hell of a lot. You can date someone three years younger, but not four. It's ironclad.

I finish pulling apart the front hub, being careful not to lose the pea size ball bearings. I dig through the contents of the toolbox, searching for my tube of fresh grease. I smile, remembering the first time I repacked my hubs. I was thirteen and just getting into bicycling. My dad suggested I use automotive grease for the hubs. Luckily, I declined. Vehicle grease, as I later found out, would attract dirt and grit in any manner possible and proceed to grind up my wheels.

It's strange now though. When I was young I thought that my father was a complete genius. He knew everything. Now he always says that I think I know everything. It's not true, really it's not. It just seems like now that I'm learning so much more, I start to form my own opinions. I'll think of different ways to do things. It's not that I think Dad's stupid. I just think he's wrong sometimes. And he does read a lot into things. Usually it's not what I say that gets me into trouble. It's how I say it. Old man doesn't handle sarcasm too well either; he did not take it well when he found out that I occasionally refer to him as Hagar the Horrible. My grandpa takes sarcasm well though, so maybe it just skips a generation.

I finish with the front hub, turning it on the axle to check its tightness. It feels right, and I move to the rear hub. Then I start the procedure again.

CHAPTER 11

I stare blankly at the television set at the front of the room. The psychology movie is hellishly boring, the narrator droning on and on about metacognition or some damn thing. I look around the room; no one to talk to. I'm glad I'm in advanced placement psychology, but being the only junior in the class isn't a whole lot of fun. Sure, the seniors are fairly nice, and some of the girls are extremely attractive, but they're not close friends by any means.

I drop my head onto the table, allowing my eyes to slip out of focus. God I'm tired. It's strange, I go to bed and wake up at roughly the same time each day, but sometimes I'm full of energy and other times I can hardly move. I guess today is one of the latter. Maybe it's hormonal. I take one last look at the television and close my eyes, hoping to catch a little bit of sleep.

The fog lifts after the final bell. As I walk out of the English room I feel better, ready for practice. Then I see her, walking out of one of the classrooms. I've got to say something before she gets too far away. Think think think...

"Hey Sara!" I yell. She turns around. Good, now why did I yell at her? Think fast, she's getting closer. "Have you studied for the chem. test on Monday?"

"No, not yet," she says, looking guilty. "I was planning on studying this weekend."

"Oh," I say, "Well, do you want to attend our study group?"

Aaaarugh! What the hell am I doing?! We don't even have a study group!

"I'm not sure, when is it?" she asks.

My mind races. I say, "Uh, it's tomorrow. Saturday night at my house."

What am I really doing tomorrow night? Will she really come to my house? What'll my parents say?

"Aww, I can't," she says, "My mom is having a dinner party and she wants me to be there. Sorry."

Yes! I'm off the hook. Now I don't have to set up an entire study group. Where did that idea come from anyway? Wait, she's looking at me funny. Aaah! I need to reply!

"Too bad. Maybe some other time then."

She nods, then smiles, and I walk smoothly away. I've got to watch myself in these situations, speaking before I think doesn't go well for me. Gotta remember that.

I grab my stuff from my locker and head for the theater. Maybe we can start on time for once. When I get there, something is wrong. The door isn't propped open. I check the handle, it's locked. What the hell?

"No practice today."

I turn around to see Aaron behind me, grinning.

"Jackson had to go to something in Minneapolis, he left during sixth hour," he continues, still smiling.

"So are you just going home?" I ask.

"Nah, I thought we could go golfing."

"Where?" I ask, looking around. He holds up two putters.

"Upstairs in the English Hall."

My eyes narrow, the thought of Aaron bowling with live chickens is still fresh in my mind. Ah, nevermind, it'll be fine. I hope.

I shrug, "All right, why not?"

We walk upstairs to the carpeted hallway. Aaron drops the putters and pulls two golf balls out of his pocket.

"Where did you get all this stuff?" I ask.

He smiles, "Oh, it just turns up." Then he shrugs off his backpack and produces from it a small plastic cup. "Our hole," he explains. As I stand watching he proceeds to set up the first hole. He places the cup about twenty feet away and drops his backpack, jacket, and gloves between the cup and me. It ends up looking like a fairly respectable miniature golf hole. "You have the honors," he says, handing me my club. I line up my shot and tee off, trying to remember my remedial introduction to golf.

We play back and forth for a few minutes, sending the golf balls careening off the doors, walls, and drinking fountains. Finally we both drop our shots in, and he wins the first hole by three strokes.

"It needs more pizzazz," I say, extracting my ball from the cup.

"You're right, how about a ramp?" he replies.

I look up and down the hall, no one is watching. I shrug, "It could work."

That's all the encouragement he needs. He piles up our jackets and backpacks and constructs a ramp of textbooks over them. All told the ramp is around three feet tall; capable on launching a golf ball a considerable distance.

"You first," I say.

He complies gladly, lining up his shot directly for the center of the ramp. I watch, expecting the ball to be airborne for a few yards and then bounce along the ground. Unfortunately, I grossly underestimate my friend Aaron.

He takes a full wind up, drawing the club to just behind his ear. My stomach drops. This does not look good. The ball is rocketed foreword with a violent snap. It leaps up the ramp and keeps going, a white streak flashing down the hallway. That's when the lights go out.

I guess I should say the light goes out. The plastic casing lets go with a pop as the little dimpled projectile charges through it at 60mph. The ball then shatters the fluorescent tube, sending down a shower of sparks and fragments of glass. I look at Aaron and everything slows down. The situation slowly dawns on him, and he throws a glance my way. I realize that it's time for me to go.

I dive for the ramp and grab my bag and jacket, while Aaron just stands there.

"Damn," he says.

"Time for my exit," I say, looking for the nearest set of stairs.

"Damn," he says, still not moving.

"Aaron!" I yell. Finally he looks up. "Run!"

I don't look back again. I half-run, half-fall down the stairs, taking them three at a time. I can only hope that he makes it. I know what you're thinking. Sure, there's always something to be said for staying to help a friend, but sometimes you have to watch your own ass first. Especially when it was his idea in the first place.

CHAPTER 12

I pull up to the building and kill the engine. I glance at my watch, then wonder what I'm doing here so early. The guy on our answering machine, Walter, said I should be here at 11:30, it's only 11:20. Maybe I'll get some points for punctuality. I sigh. I've never enjoyed job interviews, even though I've only been to one of them. The whole time I felt like everything I did was being evaluated. As these thoughts run through my head I also realize that if whoever is interviewing me is watching me right now it won't help my odds of getting the job. Very few people drive somewhere only to spend four or five minutes staring at their dashboard before getting out of their car.

I walk into the cafe, and even though I've been here before I'm still surprised by how dim it is inside. The Sportsman's Cafe is no friend to natural light. A waitress stands behind the counter, wrapping silverware in napkins. She's older, in her 30s maybe, and she looks slightly familiar.

"Is Walter here?" I ask. A man sitting at the end of the counter stands up.

"I'm Walter," he says. He's a big man, balding, with a thick, white beard. He's in his mid 50s, and he seems at home in the cafe.

"Are you the manager?" I ask.

He laughs, a deep, hearty chortle. "Manager, owner, cook, plumber, exterminator, I do it all."

I hold out my hand, "My name is William Larkin, you left a message about an interview." He shakes my hand, strong guy this Walter, then lets go.

"I've got your resume right here," he says, "Let's go have ourselves an interview." He leads me past the end of the counter and into the darkened dining room. "We only use the dining room when the place is full," he explains, "Which obviously isn't the case right now."

I chuckle, trying to act amused. He pages through my application, then stops at one page in particular. It's my list of interests and activities.

"Will these affect the hours you can work?" he asks.

I think for a moment, trying to imagine what the right answer would be. "They will some," I reply, not wanting to lie but still wanting to look good, "I have the school play in the fall and one act in the winter, so I could only work after five during the week. My family goes up to our lake cabin most weekends during the summer, so I couldn't work much then either. Other than that I'm pretty flexible."

He nods and continues to read through my application. Then he sets the pages down and looks at me. "Here's what we'll do," he says, "We'll start you out as a dishwasher for a few days. You'll get to know where things are so you can find your way around the place. Then you can work awhile as a cook. You'll find out how orders go through and how the food is made. Finally we'll have a waitress shadow you around and teach you everything else. How's that sound?"

I sit silently for a moment, making sure I understand what he is saying. "So I have a job?"

He smiles and replies, "Yep, you have a job. You'll be paid $5.15 an hour and you can keep your tips. I'll call you when we're ready for you to start." He stands up and holds out his hand.

As I shake his hand I think about what it'll be like to work here. I also wonder if all of my job interviews will be this easy. As Walter walks away it occurs to me that he looks a lot like Santa. If his beard were a few inches longer he'd be a perfect match. I probably shouldn't tell him though…

CHAPTER 13

"Three days people! We only have three days to prepare for our Sub-Section Tournament and we are not ready!" As the entire cast sits in the audience of the theater Mr. Jackson paces back and forth across the stage. "You people have to quit screwing around and get some work done around here. You have a good show, but it is not spectacular. It never will be unless we work at it!"

He keeps talking, but I quit listening. I withdraw from the lecture and follow my own train of thought. I knew the annual pre-sub section lecture was coming, I just wasn't sure when it would get here. Well, here it is, with Mad Jack raving in all his glory. I look at the cast members assembled around me. The rookies have slid down into their seats, doing their best to avoid eye contact with the raging director. Most of the veterans have done the same thing as myself, fading into their own little worlds.

Jackson does have a point though, we haven't been working very hard. A lot of actors graduated last year, making this year a rebuilding period. I suppose everyone figured that we wouldn't be all that great, so why try too hard? It's no excuse really, we should still perform to the best of our ability. Nonetheless, the loss of the seniors still hangs over us like a cloud. Last year we were doing Shakespeare, but now we're doing a silly British farce. Ah, Jackson looks like he's wrapping up, it's about time to head home.

Eventually we're released, and Allison approaches me as I'm putting on my jacket.

"You look chipper," I say, "What's the occasion?"

"I'm glad you asked," she replies, "I happen to be going on a date."

I frown at her, "Not with Griffin I hope."

She smiles, "No, not Griffin. It's a guy from St. Cloud."

"How did you meet him?"

"Amanda set me up with him. She says he's really nice."

I pause for a second, trying to sort things out. "Wait a minute," I say, "You're letting Amanda set you up with a guy you've never met?" She nods. I have a funny feeling about the whole ordeal, but I decide not to tell her. I stick to safe questions instead. "Where is he taking you?"

"We're going to see a movie and the we're off to dinner at the Olive Garden. After that we might go back to Amanda's."

Now, this guy might be a perfectly nice human being, but he's not real original. Not to judge a book by it's cover or anything, but I think she could do better. Amanda was never regarded as an excellent judge of character. Rumor has it that she dated a guy for three months until she learned that he was a convicted felon. He had a curfew because he was on parole, not because his parents said so. On the other hand it's good that Al is getting over Griffin, so maybe this will be a turning point for her.

"Congratulations Al," I say, shouldering my backpack. She just grins. I'm glad she knows what I mean. With that in mind I walk to my car, smiling the whole way.

My smile fades however, the moment I walk into my house.

"Will, before you take your shoes off go sort the recycling," my dad yells from the kitchen. In front of me sits a trashcan full of cans and bottles waiting to be sorted in the garage. A hello would have been nice.

I don't reply. Instead, I drop my bag and drag the can outside to fulfill my duties. The only benefit I receive is the satisfaction of hearing the glass bottles shatter as I hurl them into the 55-gallon drum. I return indoors considerably grumpier and much less enthusiastic about discussing the day's events.

"How was your day?" Dad asks, putting together a meatloaf for supper.

"Fine," I reply, pushing through the fridge for something to drink. Nothing.

"What happened?" he continues, prodding me for information.

I don't take the bait. Instead, I try evading the topic. "Oh, nothing out of the ordinary." With that issue settled I turn to walk out of the kitchen. That's when he stops me.

"Is that it?"

I sigh. It doesn't look like I'll be getting away that easily. I turn toward him and with a deadpan expression I rattle off the events of the day. "Let's see, we had an assignment in math, finished that in class. Notes and a worksheet in chemistry, played music in band and cards in study hall, discussions in social, more notes in psych., all capped off by reading a dull story in English. Can I go now?"

With this last comment my father's face darkens. His eyes narrow to slits and he stares straight at me. "William, I won't put up with this *any more!*"

I try to put up a feeble defense, "What? I told you what happened, what do you want?" It's like shooting at a tank with a BB gun. He counters with a full-scale assault.

"Now I know I'm not seventeen, so I don't know everything in the world," he fumes, "But I would like a little bit of respect! This is my house, and I won't have some seventeen year old kid treat me like an idiot!"

"What did I do wrong?" I ask, "What did I say?"

"It wasn't what you said, it was your *tone* Will. That 'you're my parent so you must be stupid' attitude you've been having lately.

Frankly, I've about had it! I don't need to take this from my own son. I'm just about ready to take away that car and that computer and sell both of them. You can ride the bus and buy a typewriter for all I care!"

His volley is followed by a tense silence. I need to be careful; I want to end the conversation without provoking another attack. I chose my words carefully, making sure it sounds sincere.

"I'm sorry. I'll try to watch how I say things." He doesn't say anything; he just keeps staring at me. "Can I go do my homework now?" He gives me a quick nod and I'm gone. I'll have to remember that, homework as a cop-out. It may come in handy again.

CHAPTER 14

*R*eady or not, here it comes. I sit in my car, huddling over the heating vents. I still can't believe I'm awake at this un-godly hour. I check my watch, it's 6:02AM. Mad Jack is late. It's Saturday morning, the day of One Act Subsections. If we don't place first or second out of the six plays we're done for the season, but we've improved quite a bit over the past week. I think we've got a fighting chance. A handful of other vehicles sit idling out in the cold, all being driven by the cast members or their parents.

Finally the two vans pull up to the school, one pulling behind it an old marching band trailer full of our props and pieces of our set. I step out of my car and grab my bag, then proceed to cram into one of the vans with the rest of the cast. The vans hold ten passengers apiece, but the front passenger seat is taken out of them to make them "legally" nine passenger vans. The school and its stupid regulations. I look up at the driver, and to my surprise it's not Mr. Jackson. No, instead, the driver is Thomas Malloy, otherwise known as Crazy Tom. Throughout my high school drama career I have made it a point to never ride in Crazy Tom's van. It's not that I have anything personally against the guy, he just gives me the creeps. On top of that, I've heard quite a few stories about him, some good, some bad. Regardless, I've been trying to keep my distance. Tom begins to dig under his seat as Mr. Jackson approaches the van.

"Hey Jack," Tom says, "Where's my gun?" This makes all of us pay attention. Tom rummages through the glove compartment. "Didn't the school leave me a gun?"

Mr. Jackson smiles, "No, Tom, you don't get a gun this time." As you can imagine, by now I'm a bit alarmed. Then Richard arrives.

Richard slides into the seat next to me, moving even slower than usual due to the early hour. He crams his gangly legs up against the seat in front of him and closes his eyes, trying to sneak in a little more sleep before the day ahead. Then Amanda shows up. Chipper as ever, the little spark plug has probably been up since 4:30 doing her hair, which bounces lightly as she skips to the van. Of course, she's not going to the other van. I'm not that lucky. No, she has to sit in my van. Great.

"Good morning everybody," she says, flashing a smile. "Isn't it a beautiful day?"

I look outside. Just as I suspected, it's still dark. I consider bringing this fact to her attention, but I decide not to. I'd like to avoid engaging in conversation with Amanda as much as I can. I pull my headphones over my ears and hunker down into the seat. If I'm lucky I can get some sleep and this God-forsaken van ride can be over soon.

When I wake up we're there, Grove City, Minnesota. The school sits out in the middle of a cornfield, with blowing snow swirling around its foundation. The farmland around us is barren and desolate, and everything is covered with a thick blanket of white.

The grumbling cast, including myself, disembarks and helps unload the set from the trailer. Then we lug our own gear into our assigned classroom. At a one-act competition each school has a classroom assigned to them for storage and changing into costume. The room is frigid. As we walk into it the first thing Richard does is to check to see if the window is open. The rest of the cast shuffles in, still groggy from the van ride. I check my watch, it's only 8:30. That means we have half an hour until the first performance and three and a half hours until our show goes up. It's time to do some wandering.

I grab Aaron by the arm and pull him around the corner.

"Let's go exploring," I tell him, leading him away from our room.

"What do you mean?" he asks.

"We're in a school we've never been to. I don't feel like watching the other plays. We have three hours to kill, so let's go exploring!"

Aaron shrugs, that must mean yes. We're off. We walk through the semi-darkened hallways, on the lookout for anything that might be entertaining. That's when I see it: the biology room. I walk over to check the door. Luckily, some moron left in unlocked. Those trusting fools. I open the door and step inside. Things look promising, there seems to be a fish tank in the center of the room and some type of rodent cage in the corner. Interesting. Then I realize that Aaron is still outside. I open the door to see him standing in the hallway, looking back and forth nervously.

"What are you doing?" I hiss, "Get in here!"

"I don't know Will, what if we get in trouble?"

"We won't," I assure him, "Now get in here!"

Aaron sighs, then gives in. He slips into the darkened room and closes the door behind him. I reach for the light switch, but then think the better of it. No sense in making us any more conspicuous than we already are. As I expected, a little gerbil sits at the bottom of the rodent cage. Or maybe it's a hamster. Never could tell the things apart. Well, either way, it's a little brown fuzzy guy just begging to be played with.

"Hello precious." I turn around to see Aaron talking to the fish in the tank. I wonder what would happen if Aaron was president. I push the thought away. Sometimes it's best not to consider such things.

I start poking around a bit, shuffling through the desk drawers and filing cabinets. It takes a little time to find what I'm looking for, but eventually I get to it. It sits there in the drawer, gleaming in its shiny plastic glory: The Hamster Ball.

"Aaron, come here for a minute and help me with something."

He lingers for a moment, gazing at the fish, before wandering over to the rodent cage.

"Here, help me get him into the ball," I say, lifting off the top of the cage.

"Are you crazy?!" he exclaims, taking a step back. "What if it gets away? Do you know how much trouble we can get into?"

"Relax, it'll be fine. He'll be in his little ball so he can't get away from us." Aaron still doesn't look convinced. "We'll only have him out for a little while, I promise." Aaron's shoulders slump. I knew I could wear him down. "Now hold the cage open and I'll drop the rat into the ball."

Surprisingly, the operation goes smoothly. It looks like the little hamster/gerbil/rat thing likes the ball, because he hops right in. I set the ball on the ground and the little guy takes off. He flies across the room, scampering in his little ball like a little furry convict running from the FBI.

"Aaron, the door!" I yell, pointing to the door leading to the next classroom. He arrives at the entry just in time to kick the ball away and send him away from the opening. We mess around with the little guy for fifteen or twenty minutes before he gets tired and starts slowing down. He's one tough rodent, never seeming any worse for the wear. He doesn't seem to mind any of it; even when we play soccer with him, sending his little fuzzy body flipping around in his plastic shell. When he finally does get tired we decide to put him back. He hops back into his wood chips as happily as he came out. I'm just about to leave, pleased with the entire experience, when Aaron speaks up.

"Uh, Will, you'd better come over here"

I stop at the door, "What is it?"

"I think this fish is dead."

My stomach sinks. "What did you do?" I ask, walking over to the tank.

"Nothing," he says, not taking his eyes off the fish. Aaron is right, the big fat goldfish looks extremely dead. It floats belly up on top of the water. The aerator spins it around in circles, almost making it appear to be alive. Almost.

"Was it dead when we got here?" I ask.

"I don't think so, but what could have killed it?"

I think for a minute. Neither of us put anything in the tank, all we used was the little fur ball.

"You're sure you didn't touch it?" I ask.

"Positive."

"Then it can't be our fault," I say, examining the predicament. "Let's get the hell out of here."

"Wait, shouldn't we take it out?"

I turn to face him. "What do you want us to do? I don't want to be seen walking out of the biology classroom holding a dead fish. We need to walk away, and we need to walk away now." Aaron takes one last look at the dead fish, then heads for the door. We stride out, walking at a fast clip, and trying to get as much distance as possible between ourselves and the carcass. We don't slow down until we get back to our school's room, and then we do our best to act like nothing happened.

The next bit of excitement occurs as we're getting into costume. The cast is spread out between our classroom and the bathrooms, all of us trying to get into costume in time for the make up call. That's when we hear it, the unmistakable bellow of an angry Mr. Jackson.

"All right, who the hell was in charge of the make-up kit?!"

The kit he's referring to is a large gray toolbox that contains all of our stage makeup. Without it, we look like a bunch of pale white ghosts on stage.

After his initial outburst, Mad Jack begins grumbling and kicking things around, searching for the box. The cast exchanges nervous glances, all of us trying to remember who is in charge of the kit. I'm sure it's not me. I vaguely remember Jackson mentioning something to Pete about it, but I'm not going to say anything about it. I like Pete, even though he's a freshman. If he does get in trouble I don't want to be the one that puts him there.

"Well, who was in charge of it?!" Jackson screams. "It obviously isn't here. Where the hell is it?! Is it on the vans? Is it in the school? Is it on the moon? Feel free to shout out the answers when you know 'em, because we're on stage in less than an hour!"

"The van," a voice says from the corner of the room. It's Pete. He swallows hard, then says "It's my fault, the box is in the van." I am very impressed. The kid has balls. If I got into corner like that, I'm not sure if I'd step forward. Pete gets a gold star for the day.

Jackson stares at Pete for what seems like an eternity. Nobody says a word. Finally Jackson mutters "Well, then go get it." Pete is gone in an instant, sprinting down the hall toward the doors. Everyone is stunned. Has the famous wrath of Mad Jack finally subsided? Could we be witnessing the end of an era? "What are you all staring at?!" he yells. "Get into costume!" I guess not.

Minor glitches aside, the performance goes swimmingly. Everyone hits their cues and no one botches a line. I end up feeling pretty good about the whole thing. The feeling fades, however, when Julie finally catches up with me. Everyone is packing up their costumes, wanting to see the next play of the day, when she blindsides me.

"Hi there handsome."

"Aaaarugh!" I yell, spinning around. It's like the sugarcoated voice of Satan.

"Are you coming to my cast party?" she asks. We've never had cast parties for the one act play. What is she talking about? She continues, "It should be a lot of fun. I was thinking, if you're going, maybe we could ride together. I'd be happy to drive you." This sets off warning lights across the board. The wench is setting a trap for me! Well, maybe she's not a wench. She is somewhat attractive.... Wait a minute, what am I thinking? Must resist...

"Sorry Julie, I don't think I can," I reply, looking for a way out. She pouts.

"Why not? It'll be fun"

I force a smile, "It's my mom's birthday. The whole family is having dinner together."

She perks up, "Can I come?"

Of course not you fool, my mom would hate you more that I do. Besides, it's no one's birthday; I just want you to get the hell away from me.

"No," I reply, "its kind of a family thing. Sorry."

She smiles, "Well, maybe some other time then." I nod and then turn away, hoping that I won't have to speak to her again.

As things turn out, my exchange with Julie isn't the most frightening conversation of the day. Far from it actually. The really freaky stuff comes from Crazy Tom. After the performances were finished and the awards given out, everybody piles into the vans and prepares to leave. That's when I see them. A man, a boy, and a dog are all walking through a swamp near the school. They appear to be looking for something, but I can't imagine what. Tom notices me looking at them and speaks up.

"Yeah, I've been watchin' 'em for the past forty five minutes. I think they're lookin' for the wife's body."

I look over at him. His face shows no sign of emotion. I can't tell if he's kidding or not. He just runs his hand through his uncombed hair and keeps looking out the window.

"Sure," he continues, "The old man is probably sayin 'well I had the sight lines between them telephone poles an' the farmhouse, she should be right here.' Then da boy'll say 'damn dad, we're screwed.'

Then the kid'll start whinin' an' say 'dad, I'm hungry.' The old man'll say 'well, let's eat the dog then.' 'Dad, can you cook?' 'Nope, I'll just kill 'em and you can cook 'em." Tom rattles off this dialogue with a good bit of enjoyment, adding voices and emotions for the characters. All I can do is stare.

Seeing that everyone is in the van, Tom starts it up and pulls out of the parking lot. Then he notices that I don't have my seat belt on.

"Better snap that buckle on," he says, "In a crash you'd be shot through da window like a cannonball." I buckle up, instantly regretting the oversight. "I used to work as an ambulance driver for Ramsey County," he continues, "The worst wrecks were always the ones where they didn't wear seat belts. In the ER the docs would always be yellin "QUIT SQUIRMIN"'! And the guys'd say "I'm squirmin' because you're shovin' a big metal spike in my eye." Well, that glass don't come out with a magnet, so they gotta pry it outta their eye with a hook. Then they might say "hey, it did come out with a magnet, it was just that penny you left lyin' on the dash." Tom chuckles, enjoying his own joke. I don't reply, I'm too afraid. We drive the rest of the way home in silence, and Tom doesn't say another word.

CHAPTER 15

$\mathcal{I}$t's Monday afternoon. I shuffle through my front door, tired but grateful. I have the house to myself. I kick off my shoes and drop the mail on the kitchen counter. After I pull off my coat and backpack I flip through the mail, hoping to find a magazine or catalog addressed to me. Instead, I find a letter.

I'm confused. No one ever sends me letters. It's not my birthday or anything. I flip the envelope over, but there's no return address. I can't make out the postmark either. Puzzling.

I run my index finger under the lip of the envelope and tear it open. I open the letter itself and staring back at me is a giant, multi-colored clown face. I jerk my head back instinctively. Damn Lisa Frank stationary. I immediately look to the bottom of the letter for the identity of the sender. It's from Carrie Dempsey. My head jerks back again. This can't be good.

My sporadic relationship with Carrie began about three years ago. We were at One Act Sections and I saw her in the halls. Later, one of her friends came over and wanted to introduce us. We really hit it off, and we were together for the rest of the day. I met her friends, she told me about her family, and we talked about all the things we had in common. The problem was that she lived thirty miles away. It doesn't seem like much now, but for a kid without a car she might as well have lived on Jupiter. We kept in touch afterwards, writing back and forth with the occasional phone call thrown in for good measure. She was going to come and see me once, but her ride didn't show up and she never came. Things fell apart after that. Either I didn't write, or she didn't write; something happened and I didn't hear from her for almost six months. Then I ran into her again at last year's section competition.

It was just like old times. She saw me first, and she ran down the hall and jumped into my arms. She told me how much she missed me and apologized for not keeping in touch. She said that she talked to her friends about me nonstop and that she was oh-so-happy to see me. We were together the entire day. When it was finally time for me to go she hugged me, then we kissed. It was my first real kiss, and to this day it's still a blur. All I remember is that I was elated, and that I walked onto the bus beaming.

We kept in touch for quite some time afterwards, but eventually I realized that there was no hope for a long-distance relationship. The amount of time between our letters became longer and longer, and the letters finally stopped. That was last August, and eventually Carrie was forgotten. I guess now she's back.

The letter reads as follows:

Dearest Will,

Hey! How have you been? I'm sorry I haven't written in such a long time. I've been really busy lately, trying to study for my next driver's test and attending night classes. I miss you sooo much! I know it sounds weird, but I still talk about you all the time. All of my friends know about you. January 19th was the best day of my life! We have to see each other soon! Stop by if you're in town, or else I can come to you.

So what have you been up to lately? I've been working on the school musical, "A Christmas Story". It's great, I'm in the play with some of my best friends, so we're always having all kinds of fun. Just the other day, Sean found an old Indian headdress in the prop room and we had a powwow. It was hilarious! He's always goofing around like that.

I just can't wait to see you again! We have so much catching up to do. Be sure to write as soon as you can!

Love,

Carrie

Scary. This is all really, really scary. She's been busy? She's been busy for an entire year?! I though she fell off the face of the earth, and that was fine with me. I seriously don't need this right now, really I don't. Maybe I can just ignore her. I can ignore her and she'll go away. But she won't go away. She'll just track me down. She'll track me down and she'll tell me she's been busy. Then she'll want to ask me about our relationship and how she's really missed me and how we were meant to be together. No, I'll have to reply. A clear, polite, concise reply telling here to get the hell away.

Then again, I don't really want to encourage her to reply back. What to do, what to do…

I won't reply. Maybe she'll take the hint and just go away. She was kind of attractive though…NO! Stop that! I'll ignore her and she'll just fade away.

CHAPTER 16

I sigh as I haul myself through the front doors of the school. It takes me a moment to moment to realize what day it is. Today is Wednesday. This cheers me up a little bit; I was under the impression that it was Tuesday. I'm one day closer to the weekend. A pleasant little bonus. I walk through the line and pick out my breakfast, being certain to choose the roll with the most frosting. I sit down in my regular seat, and as I open up my carton of orange juice Allison sits down.

"Hey Al," I say, hardly looking up from my meal. She doesn't reply. I look up. She sits there, fidgeting with her thumb ring. That's never a good sign. "Allison, what's wrong?"

She sighs. "Last night was one of the worst nights of my life." I just nod. I doubt things are really that bad, but I don't say anything. I'll hear her out first.

"What happened?"

"Do you remember when I told you that Amanda was going to set me up with this college friend of hers?" I nod. "We double dated last night."

"Things didn't go too well?"

Her eyes widen, "Things went horribly."

"Why? What went wrong?"

"First we all met for a movie. She introduced him to me, his name was Mick."

Mick? This guy's parents named him Mick? No wonder things didn't go well.

"The movie went well," she continues, "We held hands and stuff, and then we all went out to dinner. That went fine too, but things went downhill when we went to Amanda's house."

"Wait, hold on. Why did you go to Amanda's house?"

"She invited us over. I told Mom I was going to her house to study and stay the night. It's the only way I could go on a date on a Tuesday night."

I shrug. The thought really hadn't occurred to me. "What happened at Amanda's?"

"Things went fine for awhile, Amanda and her boyfriend were cuddling on one couch and Mick and I were just sitting on the other. Then I started getting uncomfortable. Every time he shifted in his seat he moved a little closer to me. Later, Amanda put in a movie and I went to lay on the floor."

I start to get worried. What did this guy do to her?

"Eventually I fell asleep. Later on I woke up, but I kept my eyes closed." Her eyes widen, "They were talking about me! I heard Amanda say yeah, if she were a guy she'd probably want to have sex with me too. Aarugh! I am never going to date college guys again."

"Back up. Let me get this straight. You're not going to date college guys again because Amanda would have sex with you if she was a guy?"

Allison looks at me like I am the stupidest human being on the planet. "NO! Mick was talking about having sex with me!"

I look around to see a handful of students now staring at us. Ah yes. I guess I could be the stupidest human being on the planet.

She scowls. "Men are pigs."

I shrug, "I guess I should try and defend us, but you're right. Generally speaking, men are pigs." Then I smile, "There are a few exceptions though."

She smirks, "I should hope so." She pauses for a moment, looking over my shoulder. "You know what annoys me?" she asks.

"What?"

"When people have to open their mouths to breathe."

I stare at her for a second, trying to decide if I heard her right. "Where did that come from?"

"Look," she says, pointing behind me. I am greeted with the sight of Alicia Stumpf. Sure enough, she's sitting at the table behind us; her jaw slack, exposing a shiny yellow row of crooked, misaligned teeth. She looks like she probably came from the murky end of the gene pool.

"I see what you mean."

"Idiots," she says. "Your nose serves no other real purpose besides cleaning and processing air, but there's always some moron who can only breathe through their mouth."

A different topic creeps into my consciousness. "You know, I think I would get killed if I ever tried to drive in England." I love conversations with Al. It's the only time I can be truly random.

She pauses, considering the concept. "Do you think it'd be all that hard?"

"Sure, think about it. First of all, I would have to drive a little bitty weak car that would crush like an aluminum can in an accident. Then I'd have to use those stupid little circle things instead of a plain old stoplight. And then to make it all that much worse, if I ever quit paying attention I'd probably swerve over to the right hand lane and get killed by oncoming traffic."

She nods, "I guess you're right. That, and the British are stuck up."

"Right. That has nothing to do with driving, but yeah, that too." I smile. It's good to hear her laugh again.

CHAPTER 17

$\mathcal{A}$s our director begins rehearsal I slide down into my seat and prepare for another day in band. I've been playing the bari. sax for four years now, and it's becoming ridiculously simple. As a result, I usually daze off and it doesn't carry any real consequences. My thoughts drift to Sara. I'll bet she has no idea how I feel about her. She's probably oblivious to the fact that I think about her almost constantly. I should tell her. Yeah, that's what I'll do; I'll walk up right up to her and say, "Sara, I care about you a lot. Would you like to go on a date sometime?" Sure, it's just that easy. Bullshit. I'd probably make a fool out of myself. A stuttering, stammering fool. Hmmm. A plan B is definitely in order. I suppose I could use the age-old junior high trick. I could have Billy tell Johnny to tell Suzy to tell Sara that I like her. Ugh, but I don't want to resort to that unless I have to. I need to tell her somehow, before it's too late. I don't know if I could stand it if she was with another guy.

Finally, with just a few minutes left in the hour, our band director dismisses us. I shove my music into my folder and snap it shut. I walk over to my instrument case, twist my sax apart and drop it in. This done, I try to find Scott. He sees me as I walk toward him.

"Hey Will, did you hear the news?"

"What news?"

He smiles, "The news about the underwear thief."

"What?" Did he just say underwear thief?

That's when the bell rings. Time for study hall.

"I'll tell you during next hour," he says, heading toward his locker. I mull over what he said as I walk over to study hall. Did he really say underwear thief? Why would someone want to steal underwear? Maybe they don't have enough. No, maybe it's some sort of twisted fetish. I guess I'll find out soon enough.

As usual, I'm the first one of our foursome to get to study hall. I start firing questions at Scott before he even gets through the door.

"What do you mean 'underwear thief?' What happened? Whose underwear was stolen? When did all this happen?"

He shakes his head, "Just deal the cards."

"No. Tell me."

Aaron and Paul come in midway through our exchange, both looking puzzled.

"What are you guys talking about?" Paul asks.

"The underwear thief," I reply. I turn back to Scott, "So what happened?"

"Well, here's what I heard," he says, leaning over towards us. "Do you remember earlier when they closed down the south wing?"

I nod. This morning the principal came on over the P.A. and directed those in classes within the south wing of the building were not to leave class until told to do so. I thought it was odd, but I guess I forgot about it.

Scott continues, "They were checking the classes for the underwear thief. I guess while the gym class was swimming this morning someone snuck into the girl's locker room and stole all of their underwear."

"Wait, does that mean there are a bunch of ladies running around without any underwear?" I ask.

"Is that all you ever think about?" Paul snaps.

"Yeah, I'm just trying to pick up some of the slack."

"Nope, sorry to disappoint," Scott says, "But they were all sent home."

I scowl. I had my hopes up for a minute there. Too bad.

"That's bizarre," I say, contemplating the issue. "If they haven't caught the thief, that means that somewhere a kid is running around with a backpack full of underwear."

"What do you think they'll do with it?" Aaron asks.

I shudder. It's better not to think about it. Then another idea creeps into my thoughts, "What if it's not a student? What if it's really a teacher?"

The idea hangs in the air like a cut oak about to crash to the ground. Then Paul sums up the general opinion of the group.

"That's just wrong."

The issue settled, we dive into our card game.

"First jack deals," I say, flipping the cards over face up.

As the cards fall, Scott speaks up. "Paul was telling me today how he could take over the world."

"Really?" I ask, intrigued. "Do tell." I can see it now, the choirboy who takes over the world.

Paul looks up from his cards, "It's quite simple really. We slowly infiltrate Canada for its natural resources and Mexico for its cheap labor. We then have spies or assault teams disable all of the tactical nuclear sites around the globe. Then all we have to do is use our nuclear superiority to stop any and all retaliation. To finish things off we place our officials at the head of every major country on earth. Bingo, we rule the world."

I shake my head, "Paul, you truly frighten me sometimes."

"What? It makes perfect sense?"

"When do you find the time to think up stuff like this?"

He shrugs, "It just comes to me I guess."

I smile, "That is frightening Paul, but I have something even scarier."

Scott turns to me, "Something more frightening than Paul ruling the world?"

"Yep, Julie hit on me again."

Paul grins, "She's still after you, huh?"

"Yeah, she invited me to a party she's running. I guess it's some kegger at her cousin's dorm."

Paul rolls his eyes, "Sounds like a real health fest."

"No kidding. I told her I'm busy that weekend. The next one too. I guess she talked Jeremy into going."

Scott laughs, "Jeremy Valentine? Yeah, that's right up his alley."

Jeremy Valentine is not one of my favorite people. He somehow maintains a 4.0 grade point average as well as a heavy marijuana addiction. Combined with the binge drinking on the weekends, I don't know how he gets the grades he does. Cheating can only get you so far.

The bell rings, breaking up our conversation. In the hallway I run into Bishop.

"Mr. Larkin, just the man I was looking for," he says.

"What can I do for you Bish?"

"No my friend, the issue is what I can do for you."

I pause for a second, "OK, I give up. What can you do for me?"

"I have some intriguing news for you."

"And what would that be?"

"Julie Morgan is extremely interested in you."

I scowl. "I knew that."

"You don't understand," he continues, "I mean she is enthralled with you. She focuses on you, makes sure she passes you in the halls just so she can see you; she even changed her schedule so she eats the same lunch you do."

"Where did you get all this?"

"I never reveal my sources. I have it on good authority, so I thought I would pass it along. Good day William."

With that Bish is gone, lost among the students crowding the hallway. His words stay with me, and I decide to bring the issue before the lunch table.

When everyone finally has their lunches and is sitting down, I repeat what Bishop told me.

"So? What difference does it make?" Scott asks.

I think for a moment, "Well, I always thought Julie just had a crush on me, I didn't know it was this serious. And the whole thing with Sara doesn't seem to be going anywhere…"

"Whoa, hold on a minute," Scott interrupts, "You're not considering dating Julie, are you?"

"Well, I don't know…she is pretty nice."

Paul shakes his head, "Don't do it Will. She's the embodiment of Satan."

"Paul, you think everyone is Satan," I snap. I turn my attention back to Scott, "Do you really think she's that bad?"

Scott sits back in his chair, "I'd be careful if I were you. She might just be playing you."

"You've got to admit," I argue, "the Sara campaign has nothing to show for itself."

Paul shrugs, "It's a worthwhile effort: look at the benefits."

I counter, "But the odds barely hover above %50. With Julie the odds must be where, the mid %90s?"

Scott sighs, "You can do what you want, but I want the record to show that it's against my advice."

I decide to table the issue. I'll have to sleep on it. I don't want to rush into anything too soon, but Julie is nice…not to mention the big rack. We'll see.

CHAPTER 18

"Good morning everybody!" Julie climbs into the van, peppy as ever. It's another early Saturday, the day of the One Act Play Section Tournament. I'm fairly alert, given the early hour, but I still can't take perkiness this early in the day. Julie is looking good this morning though, wearing a low-cut, fiery-red blouse that accents her, uh, features. Lately the idea of dating her is becoming more and more appealing. Actually, dating anyone is becoming more appealing.

I'm jarred from this train of thought as Julie sits down next to me. She doesn't say a thing. Instead, she smiles at me and waits for me to speak. I turn away and look out the window. What the hell am I supposed to say? I don't want to lead her on, but I don't want to push her away either. Damn paradoxes. I guess I'll take the safe route and act like I'm asleep so I don't have to talk to her. I close my eyes, and after a few minutes I don't have to pretend anymore.

I awake about halfway to Pine City, our intended destination. I twinge at the crick in my neck. Sleeping in a school van has its disadvantages. To my right, Julie has finally fallen asleep. This time I managed to get myself into Mr. Jackson's van. He's staring at the road ahead, grumbling to himself. I've been acting under his direction for the past three years, and I still don't know what he talks to himself about. I would guess it's about today's performance, but he could be mumbling about politics, or maybe his favorite type of aerosol cheese. Who knows.

I pull out my CD player and slip my headphones over my ears. Ah yes, yet another way to avoid real conversation. I press play and the sounds of The Mighty Mighty Bosstones flood my consciousness for the remainder of the trip.

As we get to the limits of Pine City, Julie wakes up. She turns to me and notices I'm awake. "Will," she says, "I've been thinking things over, and I've made a decision. I want you to be the father of my children." I'm stunned. I try to think, try to force out a response, but nothing happens. Then I feel the van change direction. I look outside and realize that Mr. Jackson has turned off the road and is headed straight for the ocean! Wait a minute…

Then I wake up.

I snap my head back and look around. We're not in the ocean, Julie is still asleep, and everything is just as it was. I sigh. Why can't I ever have good dreams about winning the lottery or beach parties or anything like that? Nooooo. I just end up with wicked nightmares or twisted dreams that don't make any sense. Sigh.

We pull into the parking lot of the Pine City High School only slightly behind schedule. The set, props, and costumes are unloaded and our bags are dumped off in our assigned classroom. As Jackson walks off toward the coach's lounge, I yell at him.

"Mr. Jackson, what time is makeup call?"

"One-thirty," he replies, not even turning around. I check my watch: it's 9:48. That leaves plenty of time for some wandering. As most of the cast heads off toward the theater to watch the other plays, I grab Allison by the arm.

"Al, come here," I say, pulling her around the corner.

"What do you want?"

"Care to go on an adventure?"

She looks around, "Like what?"

"Exploring the depths of the Pine City High School."

She shrugs, "What about the other plays?"

"The next play is a drama about the holocaust. It's not exactly how I'd like to start my morning." I don't mention that I also don't want to be sitting next to Julie in a darkened theater. Who knows what she could be capable of.

Allison and I work our way through the hallways, keeping the theater to our left. I pause for a second, wondering if Al thought to bring a map. I turn to ask her, but she's gone.

"What the hell…Al!" My voice echoes through the empty hall.

"Will, shut up."

I turn around full circle. I still can't figure out where she went. "Where are you?"

A door opens to my left. "I'm over here, come on."

I walk over to the door and notice the sign above it. It reads: BAND.

"Whoa, hold on Al. Maybe this isn't such a good…" But I stop short. The brightly lit room sparkles with thousands of dollars in instruments. Guitars from Fender and Gibson Les Paul line almost an entire wall. In another corner: Percussion Nirvana. Two matched Pearl drum sets glitter in the glow of the fluorescent lights. The rest of the wall space is blanketed with glittering brasses and woodwinds. To my left, Allison pulls a shining white Fender Stratocaster from the wall and plugs it into a nearby amp.

"Al, I don't think this is a very good idea," I plead. She's forgetting something that's very important, but she doesn't pay any attention to me. She flips on the amp and starts to play.

The thing she is forgetting is that she cannot play guitar. Allison could never play guitar. The results are not pretty.

A horrid screeching fills the room. I search for a convenient exit, wondering if I should run now or wait for the trouble to start. I don't have to wait very long.

Moments later a frail janitor bursts through. Well, he doesn't really burst. The old man doesn't look like he's capable of doing much bursting. It's more of a fast walk.

"What are you kids doing in here?!"

Al looks at me.

I look at Al.

Everything seems to hang for a moment, waiting to crash down on our heads. I decide to handle the situation. I look at the janitor's nametag: Mr. Winkelmyer.

"Mr. Winkelmyer," I say, forcing a smile, "It's us, remember? Mike and Susan. We met with you last month about tuning the instruments today, since the students are gone."

His eyes narrow, "I don't remember meetin' with nobody."

"Don't you remember? You were telling us about your daughter." Please God let him have a daughter.

He pauses for a moment. "I told you about Michelle?"

I can't believe that worked. I force a nod, "Yeah, we heard all about Michelle."

He looks around, "I still don't think you kids should be in here, but I'll go check with the office." With that he leaves. Allison quickly un-slings the guitar.

"That door," I say, heading toward a side exit. We sprint out the door and into three feet of snow.

"Christ it's cold out!" I yell. A howling wind blows sheets of snow across the vacant playground in front of us.

"Where are the front doors?" Al asks.

"How the hell should I know?" Then I spot a side entrance 100 feet down the wall. "Come on." We trudge through the drifts, filling our shoes with ice and snow. I try to wrap my arms around myself, but when it's five degrees below zero it's pretty hard to stay warm in a T-shirt.

I drag myself onto the sidewalk and grab the door handle. Locked. I turn to Al and shake my head. Without a word we turn around and keep walking. By the time we reach the front door we're both freezing.

As soon as we get inside we both walk to the heating vent near the entryway, trying to bring feeling back to our extremities. I half-expect Mr. Winkelmyer to be coming down one of the darkened hallways to look for us, but no one is around. The only sound is the applause drifting from the direction of the theater. I check my watch, the second play of the morning must be finishing up. We need to lie low for another hour or two.

"Do you think we should go back to our classroom?" I ask. I never thought I'd be afraid of a seventy-five year old man, but I don't want to run into Mr. Winkelmyer again. Al nods, and we sneak back to our room. When we get there, the only person in the room is Richard.

"What have you two been up to?" he asks, poking his head up from behind his Dungeons and Dragons book. I don't reply. Instead, I just stand inside the doorway, fidgeting. Richard smirks, "I don't suppose it had anything to do with that horrendous noise a few minutes ago."

This time it's Al who smiles, "Ah, maybe."

Richard chuckles, "Yeah, I thought so."

"One point. One lousy, stupid-ass point," I grumble as I hurl my backpack into the back of our van. As of today our high school one act play season has officially come to a close. Only the first place play from each section goes on to state, and we ended up getting second by one...lousy...point. "But Will," you might say, "second place isn't so bad." We lost to a play about Aladdin. Aladdin for Chrissake! Our theatrical drama about the human condition lost to some play about a genie with a rag on his head. It wasn't even a *good* play about a genie with a rag on his head. I hate judges.

CHAPTER 19

*K*nife fork spoon fold wrap. Knife fork spoon fold wrap. Another day, another dollar, another night waiting tables at the Sportsman's Cafe. I look across my expanse of empty booths and tables. There are only eight people in the restaurant. Four of them, including me, are working here. With nothing else to do, I'm forced to wrap silverware. One knife, one fork, and one spoon all bundled up in a napkin and ready to be set out on a table. It's assembly line work and about as challenging as brushing your teeth, but it allows the mind to wander.

I wonder what Sara is doing right now. Doing her homework I suppose. I've never seen her scrambling to finish things up at breakfast like I always end up doing. I wonder what Julie is up to. Ah yes, Julie. I still don't know what to do about her. She's been around me even more these past few days, but at least she hasn't been as annoying. I even enjoy her company sometimes. I guess our relationship is improving, but it's still confusing. On one hand I have the girl who I can't stop thinking about, and on the other is a girl who can't stop thinking about me. If I could just cram the two of them together and make one person, things would be just fine. To complicate things further, Valentines Day is next week. Two days after that is the Snow Daze Dance; no pressure there. Shit. Then I'm torn from my thoughts by a short, dirty man sitting at the counter of the cafe.

"Hey Will, how 'bout some water?"

Norm. Norman Spencer has been a charge of the cafe for almost ten years. A bipolar schizophrenic, he comes into the cafe four or five times a day. Usually he'll just have a glass of water, sit at the end of the counter, and smoke his pipe. Other times one of the cooks "accidentally" makes some extra food and offers it to him. To my knowledge he's never refused it. As I set Norm's water glass in front of him, an elderly gentleman walks in the door. Another regular.

"Hey Cliff," I say, pouring a cup of coffee and setting it on the counter next to a dish of creamers and a spoon.

"Hi there Willie, how ya doin'?" Cliff is the only person I know who can call me Willie without offending me. Why? I have no idea.

"I've been better, been worse." I reply.

He slides into his seat at the counter, "How's that girlfriend treatin' ya?"

"I still don't have a girlfriend."

"Well why the hell not?"

"Because you took all the good ones already."

Cliff smiles, "Yeah, I guess I did, didn't I?"

I chuckle. We re-enact the same thing every time he comes in, usually with very little variation. When our ritual is completed, Cliff usually turns to other topics of interest.

"So Willie, I hear you've got a dance common' up next week. Got a date yet?" Cliff only really has one topic of interest.

"As a matter of fact I don't," I say, harsher than I intended. "Not yet," I add, hoping to sound a bit softer.

"Well ya better get on it. Don't want to let all those young fillies get away from ya."

I smile. I know he's not serious, but he's not too far from the truth either. It's time to make haste.

CHAPTER 20

"I'll bet you anything the cooks don't eat this stuff," Aaron says, dropping his lunch tray onto the table. It seems Aaron has opted for the overcooked, under-chickened chicken stir-fry instead of the pressed-meat BBQ rib on a bun.

"I sure wouldn't if I had a choice," I reply, looking down at my BBQ rib. In actuality it's processed meat pressed into the shape of a BBQ rib. How sad. Sure, I could have my own bag lunch, but I never could persuade my mom to do it, and I've always lacked the time and inclination to do it myself, so this is what I get.

Scott, Pete, Richard, and Paul all settle into their respective seats around the table, all choking down their government-issue rations. All except for Paul that is.

I eye Paul's bag lunch, "How is it that you always show up with a bag lunch?"

He shrugs as he unwraps his sandwich, "My mom has always packed one for me, that's all."

If we could all be so lucky. I look around the table, "Do you guys mind if I ask you a question?" No one objects, so I continue. "I'm stuck in a bit of a dilemma. I still like Sara; I have for a long time, but Julie Morgan is really attracted to me. With Valentines Day coming up I don't really know what I should do."

Aaron is the first to speak up, "Ok, how long have you been after Sara?"

I try to think back to when I first started thinking about dating her, "Almost six months now."

"And what have you accomplished in that six months?"

"Well, we've become better friends, I know that much, but that's about it."

Aaron probes deeper, "And am I correct in assuming that Julie would be all over you if given the chance?"

I smile, "Yep, that's about right."

Paul speaks up, working around a mouthful of chicken stir-fry, "What are the odds with Sara? Still around 50%?"

I nod, "Somewhere in there."

"Oh come on, go for Julie," Pete says, leaning back in his chair, "You can forget this Sara and finally get some. Go smoke that ass."

Paul rolls his eyes, "Thank you for those words of wisdom." Pete continues.

"Honestly, why not? She's hot, she's nice, and she wants you. What else could you ask for?"

"How about someone who isn't the spawn of Satan?" Paul replies.

"Ok, hold on, how about this," I say, reaching for a decision. "I'll run one last campaign for Sara, then turn my efforts toward Julie. If she does turn out to be the spawn of Satan, I can always pull out with minimum consequences. How's that for a plan?"

"Not bad," Richard responds, "But go easy on all of the campaign and efforts talk. You're asking a girl out, not bombing a communist republic."

"And just make sure you don't get in over your head," Scott adds.

"I'll do my best not to."

CHAPTER 21

*W*onderful. It's one more day until V-Day and I've made no progress whatsoever. Don't get me wrong, I've been working at it, but things just haven't taken off yet. Sara is in this class with me, maybe I'll get a chance to talk to her at the end of the hour. At any rate, I should probably be paying attention. It sounds like my sociology teacher is getting into something important.

"...and so this week we'll be doing something a little different," Ms. Hull continues. "You and a partner will be researching a historical battle and the effect it had on those involved. On Friday you will give a presentation to the class and hand in a written report. Any questions?"

Four or five hands shoot up, all with the same question. "Will we be able to choose our own partners?" someone from the back asks.

"You might be able to choose your partners for our next project, but for this one I've already assigned the groups. Listen for your name."

With that she starts reading off the list. Williams and Larson, Harding and Stewart, Larkin and Fuller. Wait, Larkin and Fuller? I'm with Sara? This is great, I'll be able to get things settled by the end of the hour.

The class breaks up as everyone pairs up with their partner. I wander over to Sara's desk, making a point not to look excited or disappointed. Joe Neutral.

"The Herdsman's War," she says, hardly glancing up as I sit down.

"What?"

"We should do our report on the Herdsman's War. My dad told me about it when I was little. Two families got into a range war out in Colorado in the 1800s. They ended up killing almost 100 people."

I'm not too enthusiastic about the idea, "If it was such a big deal, why haven't I ever heard about it?"

"It's not my fault you didn't study up on your early American history."

I ignore that little jab and plead my case, "Why don't we just do The Vietnam War or something like that? There will be plenty of information on it and we won't have any trouble finding material. Where are we supposed to find information on the Herdsman's War?"

"We'll find it somewhere."

I drop the issue, not wanting to aggravate her any further.

"How do you want to set up the presentation?" She asks.

I seriously haven't given it any thought. Ignoring the question, I decide to launch my campaign, "Listen," I say, glancing at my watch, "We don't have much time left. Do you want to come over tonight and we can figure things out?"

"No, that's all right. I'm sure we'll have enough time over the next few days."

Damn females. I can't tell if she really just wants to finish it in class or if she doesn't want to come to my house. I decide to press the issue.

"You could just come over anyway, if you want to."

"Sorry," she says, flipping through her notebook, "I have plans."

"Really? What do you have going on?"

She starts to say something, but then stops herself, "Nothing," she says, shaking her head. "Don't worry about it."

Something is wrong here. Why won't she tell me what she's doing? Is she even doing anything? What the hell?

But before I can ask her any of this, the bell rings, leaving my questions unanswered.

CHAPTER 22

*W*hen I walk out of my 7th hour class, I realize that all I want to do is go home. I'm not interested in hanging around the band room and re-hashing the day with my friends or stopping by the cafe to check the work schedule. I just want to go home. The exchange with Sara this morning seemed to drain me somehow, and a nice comfy couch sounds inviting. These dreams are cut short, however, when I get ambushed.

"William, can we talk?"

I spin around to see Julie standing behind me. I never even saw it coming.

"Listen," she says, looking as serious as I've ever seen her. "I want you to know something. I'm really attracted to you, I have been for a long time." She gives out a nervous laugh, "I think you're sweet, funny, and attractive, and I'd really like to be your girlfriend."

She gives this little speech while shifting nervously from one foot to the other in the middle of the hallway. Meanwhile, I am dying a slow, agonizing death. Christ, now what am I supposed to do? In theory I'm supposed to say that I've had a crush on her too and that I want to get married and have kids and blah blah blah. But what about Sara? I don't know how I feel about anyone right now and this pretty girl is still standing in the middle of a hallway waiting for me to say something.

"Well, thank you." I mutter, trying to collect my thoughts. Say something else for Chrissake, don't just leave her with thank you. "Listen, Julie, things are kind of mixed up right now. I'm attracted to you too, but I need awhile to work things out. Can we talk about this tomorrow?

She nods, turns on her heel, and walks quickly down the hallway. I take a deep breath. I guess that went fairly well, considering the circumstances. I look around. The hall has emptied out for the most part, leaving a few students lingering at their lockers. I'm not sure if anyone was listening to us, or even knew what we were talking about. I suppose it doesn't really matter. The only important question is what to do now. It's time to seek council.

I catch Scott just as he's walking out the door to the parking lot. I pull him aside and then launch into it, telling him the whole story. Once I'm finished he takes a moment to digest the information.

"So now what?" I ask, hoping Scott will have at least part of the answer I'm looking for.

"I don't know man," he says, "You're in a pretty tight spot. But listen, at lunch last week you said you'd go for Julie if the whole Sara thing didn't pan out. The Sara thing hasn't gone anywhere, has it?" I shake my head. "Then go for Julie. I still don't think she's right for you, but if things go wrong you can always bail out."

I nod, he's right, I'll tell Julie tomorrow. It is Valentines Day after all.

CHAPTER 23

W ell, after last night's fitful bouts of sleep, Valentines Day has finally arrived. Hearts and roses, flowers and love, apprehension and regret. Sitting in first hour only a few feet from Sara, I can't help but feel a twinge of guilt. Julie should be in her biology class getting the rose I sent her right about now. I just hope I did the right thing.

The bell rings, and as I shuffle my books together I see her. Julie stands just outside the door, holding a long-stemmed rose and beaming at me from the hallway. I walk over to her, doing my best to act like nothing is out of the ordinary. The act doesn't go on very long though, because the moment I get to the doorway Julie wraps her arms around me and gives me a long, deep kiss.

I seem to flutter off the ground, hang there for a moment, and then get yanked back down by the realization of what just happened. I stand there for a moment, stunned. Then I hear a voice from behind me.

"Excuse me," the voice says. Then, none other than Sara Fuller pushes her way past us and into the hallway.

In comparison the rest of the day goes wonderfully.

CHAPTER 24

❀

"I still can't believe she saw the whole thing," I grumble, stabbing my shovel into the snow.

"Are you still worked up about the kissing ordeal?" Aaron asks, trying to stack up blocks of packed snow. The lunch table crew is working on a model of Godzilla for the annual Snow Daze Snow Sculpture Contest. It's also the day after Valentines Day and yes, I am still worked up about the kissing ordeal.

Then Pete speaks up. "So, was it good?"

I glare at him, "Was what good?"

"The kiss, was it good?"

I almost snap at him, but then think about it for a second. "Yeah, I guess it was."

Pete smiles, "So quit complaining. At least it wasn't all bad."

I suppose the little horn-ball is right. I guess some good came out of the situation, as superficial as it sounds. I stab my shovel into the snow and set off to seek Bishop's take on the matter.

I find him walking through the school parking lot, pulling icicles off of cars.

"Hey Bish, what are you up to?"

He looks up at me and then looks back at the icicles. "William, our ferocious monster needs teeth; not to mention a few claws." He snaps off another icicle. "But I doubt you came out here to discuss the fine points of large scale reptile snow sculpture." Very perspective that Nathan.

"I guess you're right. I've reached a moral quandary."

An icicle falls from a nearby truck.

"Bloody hell, that was a good one," Bish mutters. "Anyway, go on."

"Well, here's the thing. Julie likes me, and I like Julie, I think, but I still feel guilty when I think about Sara. It's like I'm betraying her or something."

"Are you?"

"Am I what?"

"Are you betraying her in any way, shape, or form?"

I pause for a moment, chewing absent-mindedly on my bottom lip. "I guess not, we're not committed to each other or anything like that."

"You may be committed to her more than you think."

"How?"

Bish stands and faces me for a moment. "I may be wrong, but I believe your guilt comes as a result of being mentally committed to Sara. By dating Julie in this condition you are leading her on and being unfair to both her and yourself."

I drop my head, "I feel an ultimatum coming on."

"Quite right. You must decide between riding yourself of your old loyalties and drawing yourself out of your newfound relationship. The choice is up to you."

Damn paradoxes.

CHAPTER 25

*T*aking Bishop's advice to heart, I make my decision. I'll stay with Julie, even if it means fighting off my own personal demons. To seal things off I decide to ask Julie to the Snow Daze Dance, blissfully ignorant of the fact that the decision will turn out to be the last nail in my emotional coffin.

"Of course I'll go to the dance with you Will!" Julie yells, jumping into my arms. It's a pleasant sensation, holding her in my arms, but not an entirely private one. Classmates give me suspicious glance as they walk by in the hall. I guess the secret is out once and for all.

As I walk to my next class, I feel good. I've finally started making some decisions instead of sitting back as the events that shape my life unfold in front of me. Sure, Sara's shadow is still there, but it's not quite so obvious anymore. I've made the decision to pull out of a losing race, and I'm becoming more and more sure that I've made the right choice.

CHAPTER 26

$\mathcal{M}$y sense of confidence follows me through the rest of the day, right up until I reach my front door. In the center of my doorway is a hot pink Lisa Frank Post-It. It reads:

Will,

I was in the neighborhood and thought I'd come to see you. I'm sorry I missed you, we'll just have to catch up later! Love, Carrie

A lead ball in the pit of my stomach replaces the sense of confidence. She was actually at my house? How could she have been 'in the neighborhood,' I live six miles from the nearest town. I yank the note off the door and trudge inside, throwing my backpack into the nearest corner.

"I see your girlfriend stopped by," Dad yells from the kitchen.

"She's not my girlfriend!" I snap back as I kick the snow off my shoes and throw my jacket at a nearby hanger.

"Well, what is she then?"

"My own personal psycho, leave me alone," I reply, picking up my backpack and heading for my room.

"Where are you going now?" he asks, poking his head around the corner.

I start down the stairs, "To finish my homework."

No, homework isn't much fun and I don't have a lot of it to do, but it's a convenient excuse to avoid talking to my dad. It's not even that I don't want to talk to him, it's just that I don't want to explain my day within seconds of getting through the door.

I stumble into my room and flop onto my oh-so-coveted beanbag. There's nothing like the feeling of a beanbag after a long day. Bliss. Being the dutiful student that I am, I crack open my chem. book and work for a full five minutes before dazing off. My mind wanders a bit, pondering issues like what's in my chemistry book and if I could find out how to melt door locks or something like that. Maybe I could get into Dave's locker and fill it with rabid weasels or something. Three more chem. questions and a few minutes later, I'm dozing off to sleep.

CHAPTER 27

"So tonight's the big night, right?" Scott asks as he sits at our card table.

"Yeah, I'm meeting Julie at the dance."

"Is Sara going to be there?"

I shrug. "I kinda hope not."

Paul sits down in his seat, followed by Bishop. Aaron is off on vacation this week, so Bish offered to fill his seat.

"How does this fine day find young William?" Bish asks, organizing his hand.

I give another shrug, "Not bad, I'm going with Julie to the dance tonight."

Bish glances up at me, "Have you done away with your so-called demons?"

I nod, acting more sure than I feel.

Paul speaks up, "So how are things going with Satan girl? Has she tried to steal your soul yet?"

I glare at him, "She isn't Satan and she's not trying to steal my soul!"

"I heard you guys have been kissing in the halls and stuff," Scott chimes in, "Is there any truth to that?"

"Well, it hasn't been a completely consensual thing," I reply.

"HA! I knew it!" Paul lets out, pounding his fist on the table. "She's already trying to sleep with you."

I smack his fist off the table. "Just because she kissed me in the hall doesn't mean that we're going to have sex."

Paul cocks his head, "No, but it's a step in that direction, isn't it?"

Growing tired of the issue, I change the subject, "So what should I wear tonight?"

Scott rolls his eyes, "Swim trunks and scuba gear. What do you think you should wear?"

I just ignore him, "Bish, what do you think?"

Bishop smiles, "Well, I would advise against a full tux and spats or your pajamas, but I think something between the two would be more than appropriate."

That's what's so great about having friends like these guys, you can always count on meaningful advice for your everyday issues.

CHAPTER 28

Z ero hour of V-Day has finally arrived. As I step out of my car and start toward the school, I wonder how things will work out tonight. Usually the Snow Daze Dance isn't anything to get excited about, but apparently some big changes have been implemented this year. It's been moved from our dingy cafeteria into the hardwood gym, and a DJ was brought in from Minneapolis to play for it.

As I reach the front doors I can already hear the thudding of the music from the gym. I check my watch, I'm a little more than five minutes late. Perfect. Late enough to make Julie wait for me, but not quite so late as to make her mad. Once inside, I see her waiting just outside the gym. She's dressed in a snug, fire-red dress that's tight in all the right places. I'm becoming more and more convinced that this whole thing was a good idea.

"Will!" she yells, giving me a big hug that isn't at all unpleasant. "Come on," she says, leading me into the gym. "We've already missed two songs."

I allow myself to be drug out onto the dance floor as some Bob Marley reggae piece starts blaring out of the speakers. At this point, I would like it to be known that I am of the belief that the vast majority of white guys cannot dance. I am of that majority. I try though, I really try, but it's not working out too well.

Eventually I manage to pull Julie off the floor and get her to sit down. Walking over to get us something to drink, I notice Sara. She's looking better than ever, with her hair let down around her shoulders and glitter sparkling across her chest. Then I watch in horror as David Williams walks up to her, puts his hand around her waist, and leads her out to the dance floor. What the hell?

I forget about the punch and head back to our table to get Julie. I mutter something about wanting to have a slow dance with her, hardly hearing myself. I position us near the center of the floor, making sure Sara and Dave are in full view. Julie wraps her arms around me and we rock back and forth, swaying in time with the music. It's a pleasant experience, holding her close like that…at least it should be. Instead, Sara and Dave are all I can think about. That big oaf, what could she possibly see in a guy like him?

A feeling of dread creeps over me as his hand slides lower and lower down her back. Eventually, his hand isn't technically on her back anymore. She just smiles and holds him close.

"Is something wrong honey?" Julie asks, looking up at me with big Bambi eyes. "You seem a little tense."

"No, I'm fine," I reply, hardly looking at her. I should just walk over and strangle the bastard. It may not be the most reasonable option, but it sure would make me feel better. The song ends and we head back to our table. I need to sit down and think things over. Julie runs into one of her friends on the way and stops to chat, leaving me on my own for a bit. Then I spot Dave break away from Sara and head for the men's room. Not wanting to miss an opportunity, I turn to follow.

Walking through the door, I entertain thoughts of beating the guy to a pulp in the bathroom and then calmly walking away, but I dismiss the idea quickly. Odds are the crime would be traced back to me…and he could probably kick my ass.

By the time I get inside, the cretin is already zipping up. I walk over to the sink and wash my hands.

"Hi Dave," I say, trying to act friendly and casual, everything I'm not. "You come here with anyone?"

He chuckles, "Yeah, I'm here with Sara Fuller. What about you?"

"Julie Morgan. You're here with Sara huh? Are you two dating or something?"

He smirks, "Well, not yet, but I'm not gonna let that stop me."

My smile is beginning to feel unnaturally tight on my face. I squeak out a chuckle, "Stop you from what?"

Dave doesn't reply, he just winks at me before he walks out the door. The scumbag didn't even wash his hands.

I splash some water on my face and re-enter the fray, the Cheshire Cat smile plated firmly on my face. I force myself to be pleasant, to dance, and to act like I'm having fun. Compared to how I really feel, it's one of the best acting performances of my dramatic career.

CHAPTER 29

"So what did you want to talk to me about?" Allison asks, sliding into the booth.

It's Presidents Day, and since we don't have school I decided to have Al meet me for lunch. We agreed on the Embers in town, and here we are. I stare out the window at the blowing snow, "It's the dance. Things didn't go too well."

She picks up her menu, "Why, what happened?"

As usual, I tell her everything. From the hug that started things out to wanting to strangle Dave in the bathroom, I give her the whole story.

"Dave is such a bastard," she mutters. I'm glad she shares my point of view. "I'll have two eggs over easy and white toast with jelly," she says to the waitress who is suddenly standing next to the table.

I scan the menu, "And I'll have two pancakes with strawberries and whipped cream and a large 7UP."

"…and a cup of hot chocolate," Al adds as the waitress moves on.

"Hot chocolate?"

She shrugs, "It's cold outside. So what are you going to do now?" she asks.

"I'm going to wait for my food and then I'm going to eat it."

She rolls her eyes, "I mean about Dave and Sara."

"I figured. I'm not really sure. There's nothing really that I can do. I'm with Julie and Dave is with Sara. That's just the way it is."

"Well aren't you mad?"

"Of course I'm mad, but what am I going to do, go beat up Dave? Or maybe try to warn Sara that she's getting involved with an asshole. That'll go over real well." I sigh. "There's just nothing I can do."

"Sometimes I think relationships are more trouble that they're worth," Al mutters, re-arranging the half-and-half on the table.

"Why, what's happened to you lately?"

"I'm glad you asked. First there was the whole college guy fiasco, and last week I went out with a guy from Princeton. You probably don't know him, Steve Schultz?"

I shake my head.

She continues, "Tall guy, a basketball player. The date went pretty good for the most part. We went to the movies, then out to dinner. We talked, and we liked the same scenes and hated the same actors and things were going well. Afterwards, he invited me over to his place. At first I wasn't going to go, but the conversation was going so smoothly I didn't want to go home yet."

The waitress brings us our food, interrupting us. Al mutters a "thanks" to her and waits for the waitress to walk away before she continues.

"What happened once you got to his house?" I ask, cutting up my pancake. Al doesn't touch her food.

"We went down to the basement and Steve turned on Saturday Night Live. We sat together on the couch for awhile, and then he kissed me."

"That's not so bad," I reply.

"You don't understand. After he kissed me he tried to put his hand up my shirt."

"Oh. That's not exactly the same thing."

"I pushed him away and stood up, asking him what he was doing."

"And?"

"And he said he was just being friendly."

"What did you do?"

"What do you think I did? I left." She shakes her head, "Why do I always seem to attract guys that are trying to knock me up?"

I shrug, "I guess you're just not very lucky." Our conversation moves on to other topics: time travel, the ugly uniforms the waitresses have to wear, the best methods of removing gum from one's hair, but for the rest of the day I can't help but think of Sara and that rat bastard Williams.

CHAPTER 30

*T*he following Wednesday I walk into the darkened theater to find Mr. Jackson, but I find Bish instead.

"Sir William, would you be interested in attending a social function with myself and a few of my merry men?" he asks.

I smile, "I guess that depends on a number of things."

"Such as?"

"What's the social function and who are your merry men?"

"We will be attending a musical performance at Java Z," he replies, referring to a coffeehouse in St. Cloud. "And we shall be traveling with the freshmen duo of Aaron Paulson and Pete Roden."

"Sure, sounds like fun. Let me call my parents and we'll go."

"Excellent," Bish replies, hopping down from the stage, "I'll retrieve Aaron and Pete and we'll assemble at my vehicle in ten minutes or so."

I stop by the high school office to call my parents, then head out to the parking lot. I grin as I see Bish standing by his car in the lot. Mr. Bishop drives a candy apple red 1968 Ford Mustang that he and his father restored from the ground up. It took them two years and over 300 hours of work, but it was worth every second. The four of us pile into the Mustang and we're off.

To his credit, Bish is a fairly responsible driver. Well, as responsible as you can be behind the wheel of a vintage Mustang. For the most part he drives about 15 or 20 mph over the speed limit, but when he passes, he PASSES.

"So how goes the never ending hunt for the perfect mate?" Bish asks while blowing by a semi at damn near 100.

"Not so good," Pete says, poking his head between the two front seats. "I can't seem to make any progress."

I twist around in the passenger seat so I can face him, "That's because you try to bag any girl you come across."

"So?" he says, "What's so wrong with that?"

I shake my head, "It's guys like you who give our entire gender a bad name."

"So how have things been going with Julie? Get any?"

I scowl. "Fine, and no."

"Not wonderful? Why aren't things going wonderfully?"

"Leave me alone."

Later on Aaron speaks up, leaning foreword from the back seat, "Bish! You have to turn off here on the right!"

Bishop cocks his head, "And why would I want to do that?"

"The gas station up here sells Blue Ox."

"And what, pray tell, is Blue Ox?"

"An energy drink loaded with caffeine."

"Yeah. Last time we had it we drank so much we got all shaky. We've got to get some," Pete adds. Bish turns to me.

"Any objections Mr. Larkin?"

I shake my head, "Fine by me." We pull into the convience store and pile out of the car. The freshmen make a beeline for one of the coolers and load up with a dozen or so of the tall, narrow cans. Bishop plucks a can out of Pete's arms and inspects it.

"Seems fairly harmless," he remarks, handing it back to Pete. Bish and I wander out to the car and wait for the other two. Coming out of the store, Aaron is already gulping down his first can while Pete struggles with the tab on his own. Upon reaching the car they hand a can of the concoction to both Bish and myself.

I take the first sip and wince. The taste resides somewhere between bitter Mountain Dew and soap. "We're not drinking this stuff for the flavor," I mutter.

"No," Aaron replies, finishing his first can as we pull back onto the highway, "But it sure does make the evening more interesting."

Eventually we arrive at our destination, the hole in the wall that is Java Z. A little coffeehouse nestled in the heart of St. Cloud, it seems to be the current hot spot for college and high school students. We shuffle up to the counter and place our orders: a depth charge for me, double espresso for Bish, and French vanilla cappuccino for Aaron and Pete. We settle into a large, avocado green couch near the stage and wait for the show to start.

Java Z, in addition to being a popular hangout, is also one of the more intimate venues for live music in the area. We don't know who's playing tonight, and even if we did it probably wouldn't make much of a difference. On occasion they'll bring in a big name for a weekend performance, but weeknights are usually casual affairs. I look around the coffee house, searching for our perspective performer, and there she is.

She's off in the corner by the stage, quietly tuning her guitar. The girl is tall, maybe 18 or so, with the build of a basketball player. Her honey blond hair is cropped short, stopping just above her shoulders.

"Whoa," Pete says under his breath, "Check out the chic." I turn and see that he too has noticed the attractive musician. She looks up at us and smiles. I try to pull my head in, turtle-like, staring intently at my coffee cup as my face flushes. She's really pretty.

Pete jabs me in the ribs, "Did you see that!?" he half whispers, "She smiled right at you! Go over and talk to her."

I shake my head, mumbling something about the show starting soon. The girl, apparently satisfied with the guitar, walks up a few stairs and sits down on a lone stool in the center of the stage. She slides the microphone stand down a bit and flicks the mic on.

"Hello everybody," she says softly, commanding the attention of everyone in the room. "I want to thank everyone for coming here tonight, my name is Celeste Gordon, and I'm here to play a few songs for you. This one is called Ten Spaces."

With that she begins to play. Not only does she sing, not only does she play guitar, but she's excellent at both. She's…amazing. Our crew of four, usually ripe with sarcastic comments about any given performance, is silent. Her sweet voice soars above us, and we are quickly lost in the music.

I've always thought it would be nice to date a musician. We could hang out all the time and I could help her out when she's stuck on some lyrics and she could try out her new songs on me. When she finally breaks through and tours all over the country I can be her little island of sanity that she can always come back to.

When Celeste ends the song the audience holds its collective breath, allowing the last chord to settle into place before breaking into applause.

"Thank you," she says, looking slightly embarrassed. "As I said, my name is Celeste, I'm from St. Cloud, and this is actually my first time onstage, so you'll have to bear with me. I wrote this next song after I broke up with my old boyfriend. It's called, creatively, You Cheap Lying Bastard. It goes like this."

Over the course of the evening she plays over a dozen songs, each of them remarkably honest and real. I don't say a word through the entire performance, not wanting to break the magic that she seems to hold me in. Once she finishes her set and starts to pack up her things a small crowd of admirers cluster around her. My three cohorts chatter about her performance, but I don't really say anything. I just watch her out of the corner of my eye, waiting for the crowd to dissipate. When the fans finally drift away I get up and walk over to her, not completely aware of what I'm doing.

"You put on a great show tonight," I say, slightly surprising myself. What am I doing?

She turns around to face me, "Thank you," she replies.

"Can I buy you a cup of coffee?"

"She smiles and replies, "I don't really drink coffee."

"Juice then?"

"No, thank you."

Then it dawns on me, and I realize what I'm doing. I, William Larkin, am hitting on this girl. I scramble, searching for a way out.

"Well, ah, anyway, good show and, I hope I can see you again sometime." Without waiting for a reply I turn around and walk away, disgusted. What is it with me? Whenever I settle into a relationship it's like I keep looking for a way out. What? Am I going to keep jumping ship? Going on and on until there aren't any ships left? This is the end of it. I'm with Julie, and I'm going to quit searching for a way out. Enough is enough.

CHAPTER 31

$\mathcal{I}$t's Thursday afternoon and I'm on my merry way to class, minding my own damn business and slogging through a sea of underclassmen when I see them. Trouser Snake Dave and Sara, standing close to each other in the hall, just…chatting. I'm not close enough to hear what they're saying, but I'm not blind. I can see her when she tosses her head and laughs at his little jokes. Then he leans in close and kisses her.

I think I'm going to be sick. I turn the corner, stop for a second, and assess the damages. Why the hell does this bother me so much? By all measures I should be perfectly happy, and so should Sara. We're both in mature, healthy relationships and everything is just fine and dandy. This should not bother me at all. You know what? It doesn't. Doesn't bother me at all. I'm just the same happy-go-lucky guy I've always been. La la la.

I sigh. Damnit.

CHAPTER 32

❀

I turn onto Julie's street just before 6:30. Despite my confusion about the whole situation, I've decided to go through with our first real "date:" the classic dinner and a movie. Creeping the Olds-mobile down the street, I pray that I won't have to meet her parents. I have enough crap to deal with right now, and being forced to impress Ma and Pa just might be enough to push me over the edge. To my relief she's standing at the door, waiting for me. She steps out of the house as I pull into the driveway, calling something to her parents as she closes the door behind herself. I consider getting out and opening the car door for her, but then I think the better of it. It's probably best not to raise her expectations this early in the date. If I open her door now I'll probably be expected to open the damn thing for the rest of my life.

"Hi Will," Julie says as she slides into the passenger seat. She leans in and kisses my cheek, "You're early."

"I couldn't wait to see you," I reply, on the verge of sarcasm. She flips through the radio stations as I pull out of the drive, slowly fraying my nerves.

"What movie do you want to see?" I ask, gambling. I have no idea what kind of movies she likes.

"Oh, we have to see The House on Haunted Hill," She replies, her eyes lighting up. Wonderful. A lousy, B level horror flick with no plot and mediocre special effects. I never should have asked. Then again, what did I expect, a psychological thriller? A heartwarming drama about the human condition? Nope, a haunted house. All right, so she's no cinematic genius, but she does look good tonight in her snug blouse and black skirt. I've yet to decide if I like all the attention she gets. Every now and then I notice how heads turn as she walks down the hall, and how all the little freshmen boys stop their chatting and stare. I suppose it's better than everyone talking about how ugly she is.

The ride to St. Cloud goes fairly well. It's filled with small talk about music, movies, the news, and so on. Our tastes are different, but they overlap in a surprising number of places.

We arrive at the theater 20 minutes early. In true boyfriend form I pay for the movie, the popcorn, and the drinks. One night of tips at the cafe slowly slips from my fingertips.

We wander into the theater and find a couple of seats near the back. As the lights go down her hand slides onto my knee. The previews roll and I settle into my seat, tossing back some popcorn and trying to decide what movies I want to see next time I'm in the theater. Julie doesn't seem to be quite as interested in the show. By the time the movie starts her hand has crept halfway up my thigh, and when the unsuspecting onscreen victims enter the haunted house she can probably count the change in my pocket. Either this girl moves pretty fast or I've led a very sheltered life.

As for the movie, granted, my expectations weren't very high to begin with, but it really is a bad movie. It takes more to entertain me than a handful of people trapped in a haunted house. Then again, I suppose the movie isn't the only entertainment around here. I turn to Julie, wondering what she thinks of the show. To my surprise, she's not looking at the movie at all. Instead, she is staring straight at me. I flinch, startled.

"What is it?" she asks, looking concerned.

I shake my head and whisper, "Nothing. What do you think of the movie?" She shrugs, then shushes me, squeezing my thigh. I amuse myself through the next hour or so by counting the number of times someone goes "just around the corner" and then runs into a ghost of some sort (15). I also end up with my hand on her thigh, not at all an unpleasant feeling.

After the show we walk across the parking lot to the Park Diner, a little pre-fabricated 50s style diner with some of the best malts in town. We share a the burger and fries, but I'll be damned if she's getting her hands on my malt, despite the old "feeding each other" fetish common with couples. She ends up breaking down and ordering one of her own.

"What did you think of the movie?" she asks, finishing off the last of the fries.

I shrug, "I wasn't all that impressed. You?"

"I've always loved horror movies," she replies, grinning. "I've never been able to get enough of being on the edge of my seat. Isn't it great?"

I pause for a second, not quite sure if she's talking about the movie or her extra-curricular activities. Unseen by the other restaurant patrons, she runs her fingers back and forth over my leg, answering my question. I smile and hold her hand, giving it a gentle squeeze. There seems to be a lot I don't know about the opposite sex.

I hold her hand as we walk to the car, and I even open her door for her (man I'm a nice guy). As we drive home we talk about nothing of consequence, merely idle chitchat. I consider digging into something deeper; religion, the future, something like that, but I decide against it. By the time we get to Milaca I finally realize what's missing from the conversation: conflict. Thus far we haven't disagreed on a single issue. If I volunteer my opinion on a matter she'll either agree with me or just add some superficial comment, never debating anything.

Granted, we seem to be more and more similar, but what is a conversation without conflict?

I abandon the idea as we pull into her driveway, wondering what I should do now. I stop the car, but Julie doesn't move. Christ, now I have to be a gentleman. In the back of my mind I was hoping that I wouldn't have to leave the warmth of the car. I open the door and sigh as I step into the cold, letting out a stream of vapor. As I open her door the notion of a goodnight kiss enters my mind. Usually I wouldn't expect anything on the first date, but Julie may be an exception. I walk her to the front door and she turns to me, smiling. "I really had a great time tonight," she says.

"So did I," I reply, realizing that I mean it. Then she kisses me. She catches me off guard, but she leaves ample time for me to kiss back. I can't be sure, but I think I may have even felt her tongue dance across my lips before she finally breaks away. I drive home with a smile on my face.

CHAPTER 33

"William! Telephone!" my mom yells from the kitchen. I mute my requisite Saturday morning cartoons (no, I'm not too old) and pick up the phone.

"Hello?"

"Oh Will, I've been trying to get a hold of you for the longest time, I'm so glad you're finally around! How have you been?"

I hesitate for a moment, "Who is this?"

"It's Carrie."

My stomach drops. She's got me. I can't hang up, I can't ignore her message, she's got me on the line and I'm cornered.

"It's been a long time," I manage to get out.

"Yeah, I know. I stopped by your house a while ago, but I guess you weren't around. I've been thinking about you a lot lately. Since Valentine's Day I haven't been able to get you off my mind. What have you been up to?"

"Not much," I reply, hoping to keep things short. It's a lost cause.

"I've just been busy busy busy. I'm in the school musical right now, and I've also been working with some community theater groups."

"Yeah," I add, "I've been in the fall play and the one act, and I'll probably do some technical work for the spring musical too."

"You're not in it?"

"I can't sing," I explain.

"Oh. Well, then that makes sense. Let's see, what else…I'm trying to get my book of poems published, that's coming along fairly well."

"Who's publishing it?" I ask.

"My counselor."

"Counselor?"

"He's from my church, a really great guy. He knows some publishers in St. Louis and he's seeing if any of them will accept it."

"How'd you meet him?"

"Well, back when I was in my depression I saw him once or twice a week, but now we just have a session once a month."

"You were depressed?" I ask, my voice cracking a bit.

"Clinical Depression for a year and a half. I'm getting better now though, Dr. Barker said I'm making all kinds of progress."

I hesitate, then mutter "Huh," not really knowing how to reply.

"Anyway, I was wondering, are you busy tonight? I thought maybe we could meet over dinner and catch up on things."

"Ah, sorry, but I can't make it tonight, Mom and Dad are making me clean the house."

"Maybe some other time then?"

I attempt to handle the question delicately, "Well, the next few weeks are pretty busy for me. How about I call you when I have an open evening?"

"Really!? That would be great!"

"I guess I'd better get back to work," I say, moving toward the end table. "I'll talk to you later."

"Bye Will."

I drop the receiver into its cradle. I knew it!!! I knew she was psycho all along! CLINICAL DEPRESSION! If I ever had doubts about dropping Carrie they are a thing of the past. I suppose there are some downsides to her being psycho; I don't want to push her over the edge or anything, but it's hard to beat good, old-fashioned closure.

CHAPTER 34

*T*he next day I head over to Scott's after brunch with my parents. It's an interesting custom in our house, no matter how busy we are during the week we manage to eat together every Sunday morning. Sure, it's a little Norman Rockwell-esque, but it allows us to feel like we're at least approaching normalcy.

My English folder is riding with me on this trip. Scott and I have both hacked out our English papers for tomorrow, but it's time to do some serious editing.

I get to his house, bail out of my car, and walk in the front door. The past couple of years I've stopped knocking altogether, there's really not any point to it anymore.

"Hi Mary," I say, kicking off my shoes.

"Hello Will," Scott's mom calls from the kitchen. "Scott is upstairs in the study, go on up." I plod up the stairs and go into the study. Scott is at the computer, playing Doom.

"Hard at work I see."

He pauses the game and turns around, "As always. You bring your paper?"

"Yep," I say, dropping my folder onto the desk. "But it's pretty rough."

He nods, "Mine too, but it shouldn't take too long to polish."

I smile, "We should have plenty of time then." Seemingly blessed with ample time to finish our papers, we sit down and play Doom for an hour or so. Yes, there are better computer games in the world. Yes, there are more constructive ways we could be spending our time. Yes, we end up having fun.

We eventually tire of killing demons and imps, and are forced to turn to our essays. We trade papers and go over each other's work, ready to fix anything that looks horribly out of place.

"Any new love interests?" I ask, uncapping my pen.

"Actually, yes."

I peer at him over the essay, "Do tell."

"Kate Basset."

Kate Basset, Kate Basset, I chew over the name until it takes hold, "Oh, the volleyball player?" He nods. "She's what, a sophomore?" Another nod. I try to remember what I can about her. From what I can recall she's quite attractive, with long hair and a distinctive laugh. "Not bad," I remark. "Where'd this come from?"

He sets my essay down, "I'm not really sure. Her locker is over by mine, I guess that's when I first started talking to her."

"Make any progress?"

"I'm working on it, but I haven't asked her out or anything. I'm going to her game on Tuesday."

"Need company?"

"Nah, I'll be fine. How'd the big date with Julie go?" I give him the whole story, including the change counting abilities and the big finish. "Sounds like things went well," he replies.

"I suppose. The thing is, we never disagreed."

"Isn't that a good thing?"

"I don't know, it kind of makes for boring conversations." He nods. "Oh, and I got a call from Carrie yesterday," I add.

"Really? Man, when was the last time when you heard from her?"

"Back when she left that note on my door. Get this, I was right, she is psycho!"

"What do you mean?"

I give him the play-by-play of the phone call, paying special attention to the segments involving the words "clinical depression."

"Do you think she'll come by your house again?" Scott asks.

"God, I hope not. Why can't she just go away?"

"Just make sure you let her down easy, you don't want her to go and slit her wrists or anything."

"No kidding. That's all I need, a girl I can't stop thinking about, a girlfriend who can't keep her hands off me, and a suicide risk."

Scott smiles, "What a tangled web we weave."

I shake my head, "OK, enough soul searching. How about another round of Doom?"

We never finish our English papers.

CHAPTER 35

The next day begins with a slap in the face. Sometime in the night our water heater decided to give out, leaving me to shower in a frigid stream of glacial runoff. Oh joy. By the time I get to school my cup of coffee has done its part to warm me up, especially after I spill most of it on my hand as I get out of my car. Mopping the scalding coffee off my hand and jacket, I wonder if the morning's misfortune is an omen. Maybe I should just call it a day and go back to bed. Instead, I press on.

The two hours immediately after the coffee incident go fairly smoothly, but little do I know that it's just the quiet before the storm.

The first drops of rain fall in the hallway before lunch. I always dread those few minutes of passing time, because I am forced to walk by Sara's locker. As always, Dave is there. Leaning up against the wall, all calm and collected, he rattles off stupid jokes and clichéd compliments, whisperings sweet nothings into her ear. Every single day I walk by this tasteless display of affection, and every day I walk by quickly and then go on my merry way to lunch, except for today.

No, today Dave breaks away early for some reason and ends up walking to the lunchroom right by my side. A sucker for punishment, I open up the lines of communication.

"You're still with Sara I see."

He smiles, "Yeah, goin' on a month now."

"You doing anything special?"

"Well, I'm taking her out to dinner," his grin widens, "but I don't think we'll go straight home."

I squeak out a chuckle, "What, are you headed off to a gravel pit or something? Going to drive into a cornfield and run out of gas?"

"Nah. A hotel."

My jaw clenches instantly. That bastard. I force myself to tiptoe around the issue, trying not to look too interested. "Are you sure she's ready for that sort of thing?"

"More than ready," he replies, "She probably can't wait."

Dave is then unable to speak, as I smash my fist through the front of his mouth, lodging a few teeth into the back of his throat. He drops to his knees, choking on the blood flowing from his mouth and tongue.

"How do you like that?" I say, kicking him in the gut. He chokes, gagging on blood. "Now you listen here. Stay away from Sara, or else you will feel my wrath once again."

"She probably can't wait."

I take a deep breath and try to unclench my fist. Smashing Dave's teeth through the back of his throat does sound appealing, but I'm sure it would carry considerable consequences. "I don't know man," I say, shoving my hands into my pockets, "I'd be careful if I were you."

He tips his head, "You seem pretty interested in all this. Anything I should know?"

My cover broken, I decide to open up a bit. "You know, you should treat her with a little more respect."

He stops and turns to face me, "And what was that Will, a threat? A command?"

I clench my jaw, "A strong suggestion."

"You don't fool me Larkin, I know you've been after Sara all along." I stand still, not agreeing, not disagreeing. He continues,

"The thing is, you blew it. You're done. I'm with Sara, and there's nothing you can do about it." With that he turns on his heel and leaves. I stand in the middle of the hallway, dumbfounded. Angry with myself for not saying anything, not retaliating in any way, shape or form, I go off to the commons to sulk. I don't feel like eating anymore.

CHAPTER 36

The conversation with Dave eats at me for two days, forming a hardened ball of anger in the pit of my stomach. By the end of the day on Wednesday I decide to do something about it. I approach Sara after school when she is alone in the hallway, after Evil Dave has gone off to lift weights.

"Hey Sara," I say, trying to sound as casual as possible, "Can I talk to you for a minute?"

"Sure," She says, checking her watch, "I've got a couple of minutes. What's up?"

"It's about Dave."

"What is it? Is he OK?"

I nod, slightly put off by her concern. She really seems to care about the dirt bag. "He's fine. It's not anything like that. I was just wondering if things are all right between you two."

She looks puzzled, "Things are fine, why?"

I pause, trying to collect my thoughts. "I was talking to him the other day and I was worried that you might be going too fast."

She takes a step back, "You know what Will? That's none of your business."

I raise my voice to match hers, "Sara listen, I care about you and I don't want you to end up getting hurt."

She takes another step away from me, "Is that what this is all about? That you care about me?" Now she's almost yelling, "I am perfectly happy with David and we are fine!"

I soften my voice, trying to calm her down, "I'm just worried that he's trying to use you."

"I don't see why it's so hard to believe that David is nice and kind and caring and that he makes me happy."

It is only now that I realize I am in a losing battle. "I'm sorry," I murmur. Then I cut my losses and walk away.

Psychologists say that acceptance is the last step in mourning the death of a loved one. The same is probably true for lost relationships. I guess I haven't gotten there yet.

I spend the rest of my week stewing in my own special blend of anger, jealousy, and self-pity. Most of my friends seem to understand. Most of them keep their distance, and a select few try to help out, even though I am not exactly a big 'ol ray of sunshine. It's good to have friends at a time like this.

CHAPTER 37

*U*nfortunately, my friends are not there to help me today. Today my darling father decides that all of the dead trees that seem to multiply in the woods around our house are ugly and need to be removed. I, of course, must assist him in this task.

Dad kicks me out of bed bright and early, wanting to "get started right away." I don't bother to take my time getting ready; stalling won't do any good. I am beginning to view father-son projects as Band-Aids on leg hair; get it done quick and it might not hurt as much.

Now you may be wondering, why would one want do all of this hard, physical labor, especially while trudging through snow in the middle of winter? It is because my father is not afraid of work, tractors, or chainsaws. I actively avoid all of them. First of all, I'm not exactly an outdoor labor, sweat and blood, shoulder to the grindstone kind of guy. I don't like tractors because I seem to have an unnatural tendency to run them into things. And finally, chainsaws. I honestly can't see how anyone can't be afraid of chainsaws. The whole loud engine, moving blade, ability to hack off arms and legs thing gets to me every time.

I walk outside to find Dad already in the garage, pouring gas and oil into the chainsaw.

"You ready?" he asks.

I sigh, "As ready as I'll ever be." That seems to be enough, as he starts for the tractor, carrying the chainsaw. He fires up the old, beat up John Deere and we rumble down the driveway. As I ride along, I noticed the numerous limbs and trees that have already been marked with blaze orange fluorescent tape. Dad was up earlier that I thought.

The process is fairly straightforward. Dad trudges into the woods and cuts down any dead limbs or trees, I haul them back to the tractor and load them up. Once the bucket of the tractor is full we haul the wood elsewhere into the woods and dump it onto an ever-growing woodpile.

To my credit I think I handle things pretty well, given the circumstances. I haul the wretched logs with a minimum of griping or whining. Things go south, however, when he tells me to drive the tractor.

"No way," I say, shaking my head, "I'm not doing it."

"Oh quit it," he replies, "you could use the practice." He points at the tractor, "Now sit down."

I stand my ground, "I'm not going to."

"Damnit Will, it's not going to bite you. Now sit the hell down."

I don't move.

He finally gives in, muttering something as he gets on to the tractor. I don't quite hear what he says, but I catch enough hard "k" sounds to know he's not very happy.

The next twenty minutes or so are spent drenched in a tense silence. We unload the wood from the tractor, then go back down the driveway for another load. When Dad stops the tractor he pauses and looks through his pockets, searching for something.

"Have you seen my gloves?" he asks. I shake my head. "I must have left them back at the woodpile. Run and get 'em." I take a long glance down the driveway and let out a deep sigh. Why do I always have to be his slave? I slowly begin to climb off the tractor when Dad yells, "Oh quit it!"

"I look at him with honest surprise, "What? What did I do?"

"I ask you to do one little thing and you act like I'm asking you for a kidney. If it's that big of a deal I'll just go get 'em myself."

"I just don't see why I always have to do your dirty work."

"Dirty work? Will, I ask you to help me with something like maybe once a month. If you were born on a farm the work would have killed you by now. Get over it and get my gloves."

Defeated, I turn and jog off to fetch his gloves. I slow down as I go from the driveway to the trail, doing my best not to trip and go sprawling into the snow. As I walk I consider what I could have said, what I could have argued back, but nothing comes to me. It looks like the old man gets another point on the argument scoreboard.

CHAPTER 38

The following week goes by in a blur. Most of my time at home is spent getting ready for our family's yearly pilgrimage to Arizona. My father's parents live in Minnesota in the summer and go down there in the winter. Our family has gone down to visit them for a week each February for as long as I can remember, and it serves as a nice way to break up the long winters up here.

The week in school is shrouded with a fog of busy work; in every class I end up doing pointless worksheets and assignments. Things get interesting, however, when chemistry class rolls around on Wednesday.

We've been looking forward to the lab experiment for the past week or so, and it has finally arrived. Lab safety has been stressed, since we're dealing with the rate of combustion of a variety of substances. This time around my lab partner is Lindsey Boyer, a small, bookish girl with a knack for numbers. The class handles things fairly well, but the fireworks start once our chem. teacher leaves the room.

Sensing an opportunity, a group of football players in the corner of the room decide to try their own experiment. The brain trust grabs a few dozen sparklers from the lab equipment drawer and furiously begin to scrape off the black substance coating the metal rods. In itself that's not a big deal, each of the lab groups, mine included, did the same thing with one sparkler in our own experiment. The scary thing is that this crew has filled an entire beaker with the substance. It gives me a funny feeling in the pit of my stomach. As Mrs. Jamison walks into the room one of the idiots throws in a match.

The explosion startles everyone in the room, causing even myself to jump a bit. The tower of flame blows through the suspended ceiling, blackening the corner of the room with smoke. By the time anyone realizes what has happened, Mrs. Jamison has already grabbed a fire extinguisher and has put out the offending beaker. Panting, she turns to the four geniuses who began the fiasco. "That," she says, "Was not a good idea."

After considerable debating between Mrs. Jamison, the police liaison officer, and the principal, punishment is eventually given out. The offending parties are forced to pay for the damaged ceiling tile, serve a week of detention, and, what's worst of all, they are obliged to watch Mrs. Jamison's hellatious kids any morning she comes into school early. Those poor, stupid souls.

The situation with Julie has remained pretty much the same, she's still extremely friendly toward me in the halls. It's almost embarrassing to have her all over me in public, especially when Sara's around. Scott continues to chase after Kate, but I'm not sure how far he's getting. I'd like to help the guy out, but I doubt my assistance would be appreciated. I really do hope things will go well for him. For as long as I've known him, Scott has never had a girlfriend. It's not that he hasn't tried, it's just that things haven't quite gone his way.

I'm looking forward to the Arizona trip, this year more than ever. I guess I just need to get away from all of this for a little while. Away from the cold, the snow, the busy work, Julie, Sara, and away from being forced to scrape my windshield every morning. I need a vacation.

CHAPTER 39

❀

*M*y bags may be packed, but I'm not out of the woods quite yet. It's Friday night, and I've got another date set with Julie. I'm starting to get more comfortable with her physical advances; this little excursion may turn out to be downright enjoyable. I pick her up at her house, once again avoiding her parents, and we drive over to the bowling alley.

As we walk in we are assaulted by the smells of cigarette smoke and beer nuts, but she doesn't seem to mind. We both get our brutally ugly shoes from the attendant behind the counter. As Julie leans over to tie her shoes, I notice she has decided to wear a thong for our evening on the town. Interesting.

We find a couple of bowling balls and get a lane. The place is nearly empty; the only other bowlers are a group from one of the Monday night leagues getting in a few practice rounds.

I start the evening out with a strike. "He shoots, he scores!" I yell, throwing my arms up into the air. I sit down next to Julie at the scoring table, "What'd you think of that?"

She gives me a little scowl, "I wish you wouldn't do that."

"Do what?"

"Be so loud. There are people around." I shrug. I don't see why it's such a big deal She flashes me a grin. "Don't worry, I'll make it worth being quiet," she murmurs, then kisses her way around my earlobe.

Wow. She probably goes up and bowls a frame, but I don't pay any attention; I'm still recovering my wits from the earlobe thing. Wow.

"You're turn dear," and another ear nibble.

I get up and throw a pair of gutter balls before I get my head on straight.

"When do you leave for Arizona?" she asks, tallying up our scores for the past couple frames.

"Our plane flies out late Saturday night."

"And when do you get back?"

"A week from Sunday, pretty late if I remember right."

She pouts, "Why the late nights?"

I shrug, "We always fly coach so we can afford to make the trip every year. I guess we get better fares if we take the red eye."

"You poor thing."

I give another shrug, "Go bowl."

We finish off our round, both ending with fairly disappointing scores (partially as a result of the earlobe thing). We hand back our ugly shoes, I pay our bill, and we're on our way. I consider taking her over to the Sportsman's, but then I decide against it. Rumors are rampant enough in that place, no sense in adding fuel to the fire. I settle on Pizza Hut instead.

We walk in and slide into a booth. This time she sits next to me instead of across from me, making conversation a bit awkward, but physical contact plentiful.

"What do you want to get?" I ask, flipping open a menu.

"Whatever you want," comes the reply.

"How about a Hawaiian pizza?"

"A what?"

I sigh. Some people are simply in the dark as to what tastes good. "A pizza with pineapple and Canadian bacon."

"Oh," she replies, her voice dropping. "That's fine I guess."

"Do you want something else?"

"No, that's all right."

What's this, a hint of conflict? "Do you want something else? Pepperoni? Sausage?"

"No," she says, shaking her head. "That's fine."

I press the issue, "We can get anything you want."

"No, that's fine," she says, pushing the menu away. She's starting to get mad, so I don't reply. I feel a little twinge of satisfaction though. At least she has an opinion about something.

Dinner is passed with more chitchat. Julie eats her pizza with neither pleasure nor disgust; hiding her feelings, if any, regarding the matter. Afterwards I driver her home, not really sure if I want the date to end or not.

"Do you want to come inside?" she asks as we pull up the driveway.

Good question. "Sure," I reply. As we go inside I notice that the house is completely dark. "Where are your parents?"

"Oh, them?" She says, flipping on the hallway light, "They're off at a dance production in the cities. We have the house to ourselves."

I hesitate. "Maybe I shouldn't come in."

"Don't worry about it. They're staying at a hotel tonight, so they won't be back until tomorrow afternoon. Come on."

I pull off my shoes and follow her downstairs to their entertainment center. She drops onto the couch and motions for me to sit next to her. I willingly oblige. She flips on the TV to something, but I don't really pay much attention; she has once again started working on my earlobe. Yes, I'm sure it sounds odd, but still…wow. Her hands begin to move a bit, over my knee, my chest, and my inner thigh. That's where I decide to draw the proverbial line, as much as it kills me to do so.

"Watch it now," I say, gently moving her hand away.

"You don't like that?" she asks, giving me a sly grin.

"It's not that," I assure her, "It just seems like we're going a wee bit too fast." She looks at me like I'm speaking Klingon.

"There's nothing wrong with enjoying ourselves," she replies. Then she starts working her way down my neck. I am torn, at a loss as to what I should do. After a quick but violent battle my conscience wins out and I stand up.

"It's getting late," I say, pretending to check my watch. "I really should get home."

She pouts. "Don't go yet, please? Just stay a little while longer."

I take a deep breath, giving my conscience enough time to overcome the rest of me one more time. "No, I really need to go." I kiss her goodbye and leave quickly so I don't have time to change my mind. I spend the drive home flipping through radio stations, both congratulating myself on my decision and mad at myself for it at the same time. Either way I seem to finally be out of the woods, for a while at least.

CHAPTER 40

I try to sleep in as late as I can on Saturday, knowing that the late flight will screw up my schedule. I spend my few remaining morning hours watching cartoons and expending as little energy as possible. By the time I summon up the willpower to finish the last of my packing my parents are already on each other's nerves.

"Jesus, what did you put in these things?" Dad asks as he hauls Mom's bags up the stairs.

"Nothing much," she says, rifling through her purse for the plane tickets, "Just my clothes."

He unzips the bag and looks through it. He pulls out two ten-pound dumbbells. "I think *these* can stay behind."

Mom protests, "How am I supposed to work out after my morning run?"

"You'll live," he mutters, tossing them aside.

The protest continues, "Why do you think you can just pull my things out of my bags?"

He spins around, "When I carry the damn thing I get to decide what's in it!" With this Mom goes back to digging in her purse, letting the issue drop.

Mom makes huge sandwiches for lunch, trying to clean out the last of what may go bad from the refrigerator. We end up eating about 4pm, most of us engrossed in some section of the daily newspaper. I glance at the weather, it looks like things will be nice for our stay down south; mid 70s without much chance for rain.

Soon enough, it's time to leave. We load up the car with bags and suitcases, filling up the entire trunk and most of the back seat. I cram myself into the back, packed in between the door and my father's immense duffel bag.

I'm silent for the majority of the car ride. I lie up against the duffel, half-acting like I'm asleep. I watch as we slide by piles of snow and ice, barren trees and icicle encrusted rooftops. It's odd to think that in less than twelve hours I'll be in seventy-degree weather. I allow my mind to wander, not really focusing on anything in particular. Even when given free reign, my little clump of gray matter still chooses to dwell on Sara and Julie. This vacation will be good for me, I'll have a little time to get myself together and figure out what I want. Once I know that, I might even decide how I plan on getting it.

I wake up as we pull into the long-term parking lot, realizing with a start that I had fallen asleep. It's 6:30, more than three hours before our flight leaves. I hope the gift shops are open. I shoulder my backpack, faltering half a step due to the weight. There are some downsides to being pulled out of school for a week. As Mom and Dad sort out their suitcases and golf bags I grab my single duffel and step back a few feet. With a little luck I won't have to carry anything else.

"Will, come here," Dad growls. Damn. I walk over to the car. "Here, carry these," he says, shoving one of the golf bags into my arms. He then picks up two more bags and heads off toward the terminal. I sling the golf bag over my shoulder, grab my duffel, and hurry to catch up.

Check-in goes smoothly. Familiar with the procedure, we get through it without any trouble. Then we come to my least favorite part of air travel. There isn't any reason the metal detectors should bother me, really there isn't. I'm not loaded with explosives, I'm not packing heat, I don't use a boot knife, so I really shouldn't be worried. Nevertheless, it gets to me every time.

As we take our places in line my palms begin to sweat. When we're fifteen feet away and I can see the cops with their uniforms and guns the rest of me starts to sweat. I didn't even know I had pores in my knees. I'm nearly shaking when the guy in front of me goes through, and then it's my turn. I'm sweating, shaking, and when I nearly run through the metal detector I probably look like the most suspicious guy in the world.

It doesn't go off. I finally exhale as my backpack goes through the x-ray machine, also passing without a hitch. It's nice to be able to breathe again.

The international terminal ant the Minneapolis/St. Paul airport is a newly remodeled facility with numerous restaurants, gift shops, and a Starbucks. We are not at the international terminal. Since we are taking a charter flight we're over at the Hubert H. Humphery Terminal, which has vending machines, restrooms, and a public newspaper. The restrooms are closed for cleaning.

I spend the next hour or so reading a book borrowed from my Dad, Rainbow Six by Tom Clancy. It's an involving book, occupying me to the point that I don't even notice the girl until I pause between chapters.

She's about my age, sitting ten or fifteen feet away from me with her mother and sister, flipping through a magazine of some sort. Her chestnut hair is cut short and held in place by all manners of clips and pins. She's wearing a vintage leather jacket over a snug white T-shirt and equally tight jeans. Someone like that probably couldn't be more out of my league if she tried.

I turn back to my book, content with elite Spec Ops teams and terrorists, when a what-if enters my mind. What if I did go over and talk to her? Honestly, what's the worse thing that could happen? She'd tell me to go away and I'd be no worse off than I am now. It might be a slight blow to my self-esteem, but I'll probably never see her again so it wouldn't make any difference. I try to muster up the courage to go over and talk to her when the first boarding call begins, ending my adventure before it starts.

I would like to say it's an interesting flight, but I'd be lying. I've flown enough so that the excitement of air travel is lost on me, and I can't even see vintage leather jacket girl from my seat, so there's no excitement there either. Most of the flight is spent reading, sleeping, or snacking on little bags of peanuts that end up being a bitch to open.

It's 1am local time when we get to Phoenix, 3am in Minnesota. It's another hour before we get packed into our rental car, a charcoal gray Chevy Lumina. I'm asleep again by the time we hit the freeway.

The arrival at Grandma and Grandpa's goes by in a blur. There are hugs, a bit of unpacking, a bed, and sleep.

CHAPTER 41

I awake to the sounds of mourning doves singing, pulled from my
sleep by a single, insulting beam of sunlight. The last of the desert
cold is cooking from the air, slowly warming the screened porch in
which I lie. A soft clanking drifts in from the kitchen: breakfast. It's
time to get up.

"Oh, good morning William," my grandmother says as I walk into
the kitchen. "Ready for breakfast?" Grandma is a tiny woman, five
foot nothing with a slight build, but she still plays golf three times a
week and bakes cookies every time her grandchildren are in town.
She's a good grandma.

"Where's everybody else?" I ask.

"Your father and grandfather are in the living room reading the
paper, and your mother is out for her run. How would you like your
eggs?"

"Scrambled please," I reply as I head to the living room to track
down the comics.

After breakfast with the family I take my customary walk down to
the neighborhood Safeway. The walk serves two purposes. It allows
me to enjoy the bright, sunny morning, and it allows me to buy
Jones Soda. The Jones Soda Company is a bit of an anomaly. It's a little soda company out of Seattle with flavors like "Pink" and "Fu-Fu

Berry." They hardly do any advertising and, which is best of all, each bottle in any given store has a different photo on the label. Unfortunately, there isn't a store in the State of Minnesota that carries the sweet nectar, so I must wait until our trip to the desert to get my annual Jones fix.

As I step into the Safeway a cool breeze reaches out and smacks me in the face. I head straight for the soda cooler, making a beeline for my Jones. On my way I walk by a dozen or so elderly men and women. Sun City is a planned community that was built in the 60s, and it is purely a retirement town. No one under the age of 65 is allowed to own property or even stay as a guest for more than two weeks. It is not a very good place to pick up chicks. I finally get to the cooler of Jones and pause for a minute, admiring the labels. Eventually I select a bottle of "Pink," one of my favorites. I consider getting a few more, but realize I don't want to carry them around on my walk. Maybe I'll stop by later. I go to the register and pay the elderly cashier before continuing on my journey.

As I stroll around the nearby golf course I open up the bottle and look under the cap. "Thank you for purchasing Jones Soda" says the fine print. A very polite bottle of soda indeed. I take my first sip. "What does pink taste like?" you ask. It's had to explain. The closest I can come to is, well, pink. It tastes like pink.

I spend the rest of the morning wandering around, checking into stores and generally wasting time, but enjoying myself all the same. In the afternoon I end up going on a little trip with Mom. After lunch the two of us hop into the rental car, leaving Dad and Grandpa to their naps, and head off to the Cactus Man. The Cactus Man is a little spot off the beaten track that sells all manners of cacti. From a 20ft. saguaro to a one-inch barrel cactus, they have it all.

When we arrive we both go our separate ways, Mom to the pottery corner of the store and myself to the potted cacti region of the establishment. I've tried to grow things in the past; plants, flowers, trees, but the only things I can seem to keep alive are cacti. It doesn't take long before I find what will soon be the next addition to my cactus garden. He's a little green barrel cactus only a few inches tall, and he costs a whopping three dollars. I think I'll name him Fred.

CHAPTER 42

❀

*A*fter breakfast the next morning Dad and I repack our bags and load up the Lumina. It is time again for our father/son road trip. Every year or two we leave Mom to her golf game and we take to the road. This time we're traveling around the rim of Arizona. Phoenix and its suburbs basically lie in a large valley at the southern end of the Rocky Mountains. For our trip we're going to drive around the rim and through the edge of the Rockies.

As we slide out of Sun City Dad kicks the Lumina up a bit, pushing 70 in a 55. He trolls through the radio stations, not stopping until he finds a local oldies station. The sounds of Diana Ross and the Supremes fill the car as we drive off toward the mountains. Then comes the bonding.

"How are things going between you and Judy?" he asks.

"Julie, and fine."

"You have the wedding all planned?"

I roll my eyes, "No Dad. I'm not marrying Julie."

"Why not? She sounds like a nice girl."

"You've never even met her."

"But you wouldn't marry her?"

I shake my head, "I don't think so."

"No chance at all?"

I sigh, "There is a two percent chance that I'll marry Julie."

He shrugs, "So dump her."

"What?"

"Dump her. If you're sure she's not the one, let her go. Date someone else."

I turn and stare out the window. "I'm not dumping her; it's not that simple. You wouldn't understand."

"I have all kinds of time," he replies, "Try me."

I shake my head, "No, it's just…too complicated." With that I turn up the radio, effectively putting an end to the conversation.

The dry desert landscape gives way to brushy steppe as we drive into the foothills of the Rockies. The cacti fade as scrubby pines and other shrubs take hold. Higher still, the land gets greener and colder, breaking into thick pine forests. The car ride is far from silent, but Dad no longer tries to dig into anything personal. Smart guy.

We stop for our first night in Winslow, about an hour out of Flagstaff. We decide to stay at the Sagebrush Motel, dropping down $40 for a double room.

I walk into our room and am slightly startled. The room looks like it was pulled straight out of the 60s. Orange shag carpeting, glass drawer pulls, and vintage ceramic faucet handles are all part of the décor.

"When are we?" I mutter, tossing my bag into a corner.

"It's all from the late 60s," Dad replies, looking over the bathroom. "But it looks like it was cleaned by June Cleaver. The place is spotless."

We settle into our home for the night, partially unpacking our bags before lying down to catch a little evening cable. Once the light is out and Old Man's snoring begins, I stare at the shadows on the wall and think. I wonder what Sara is doing right now, and if Evil Dave ever got his filthy claws on her. I wish I had some way to save her. Eventually I slip into a fitful sleep, plagued with dreams of Sara crying with him hovering over her like a demon. I wake up tired.

CHAPTER 43

*D*ad and I walk across the parking lot to a nearby Perkins for breakfast in the early morning twilight, myself still a bit groggy due to the early hour. I talk very little as we eat, devoting all my energy to gorging myself with french toast and syrup. Then we hit the road. We drive through the sandstone bluffs of Flagstaff, some of them still capped with snow, before we reach our next stop in Jerome.

Jerome is an old copper mining town in the foothills of the Rockies. Rather, it was an old mining town in the foothills. The copper dried up in the mid 40s, effectively killing off the town's livelihood. Now Jerome is primarily a tourist trap. The old mine has been renovated into a museum, and most of the old feed and seed storefronts have been turned into art galleries or coffee shops. Dad decides to forgo the art and coffee, opting instead for the museum. By the time we arrive it's almost one in the afternoon, and the sun is starting to bake down on our necks. We pay our $3 admission and enter through the mining company's wrought-iron gates.

I am not impressed. The so-called museum is a collection on ancient mining equipment slowly deteriorating in the desert heat. Displays and reading materials are few and far between, and the educational experience is far from enlightening. All I manage to find out is yes, Jerome was a mining town and yes, the mine ran out and the town died. My father, the all-knowing master of trivial knowledge, fills me in on some other bits of information. He explains how canaries were used to check for levels of CO_2 and other gases in the air. The canary, being more sensitive to the gases than humans, would keel over and die when the levels became dangerously high; warning the miners and allowing them to get to safety. He also enlightens me as to the methods they used to mine and purify the copper, as well as to the purpose of most of the pitted equipment that litters the grounds.

"Enough," I say, stopping under one of the few trees. "I seriously don't care anymore."

Dad pulls off his baseball hat and wipes the sweat from his forehead. "I guess you're right, the museum is a bust." Finally free from acting like we're interested, we turn for the door. Tired of trying to absorb any more culture, we stop for malts at a nearby McDonald's, the sure-fire culture buffer.

Leaving Jerome behind, we take off toward Wickenburg.

"Where do you want to stop next?" Dad asks, throwing me the travel guide. I stare at it for a second, debating on weather or not I have the energy required to pick it up. Eventually I comply, picking up the book and flipping to the page regarding Wickenburg.

"How about the Cinema 6?"

"What's that?"

"A movie theatre," I reply, "A nice, cool, air conditioned movie theatre."

"What kind of a road trip is that?! How about this, Wickenburg has a cowboy museum, why don't we go see that?"

"A cowboy museum?"

"Sure. A museum about cowboys and this area of the old west," he explains.

I roll my eyes, "Sounds exciting."

"Next stop: The Cowboy Museum of Wickenburg," he says, ignoring my sarcasm.

As we near the city I learn that Wickenburg is a boarder town. It marks the boundary of the mountains and the valley. The vast, arid ranches on one side and the parched desert, teeming with housing developments, on the other. Wickenburg has both a health spa and a monthly rodeo.

The cowboy museum exceeds my expectations by far. The exhibits are informative and well thought out, and some of the artwork is amazing; the gristled men in the paintings look like they're going to step out of the frames and shake my hand. Despite my efforts against it, I end up enjoying out trip to the museum. Afterwards, being in a cowhand sort of mood, Dad decides on a local steak house for dinner.

"So, what did you think of our mini road trip?" Dad asks once we put in our orders.

"I guess it wasn't too bad," I reply, unwrapping my silverware, "But it was a lot of driving. Actually, not even driving, just riding."

"Trust me, I'd like you to drive, but you can't."

"Why not? All those hours in the passenger seat are getting a little old."

"Rental restrictions. It costs a lot more to have a seventeen year old driving a rental car."

I shrug, "I suppose so."

"What was your favorite part of the trip?" he asks.

I think for a second. Nothing from the trip stands out as being really great; right now I just want to get back to Sun City. "Probably seeing all of that country," I reply, trying to sound interested. "Some of it was really beautiful."

He nods, "Yeah, maybe we should take a trip back to the Grand Canyon next year." We were up to the canyon when I was eight or so. I still have pictures, but I don't remember much of it. All I can recall about the canyon itself is that it was a really big hole and I was worried about falling into it. I guess I wouldn't mind going back.

Soon afterwards our food comes and we slip into silence, our talking replaced by chewing. We drive back to Sun City in the dark, me either sleeping or just acting like it, Dad listening to oldies. We get to Grandpa and Grandma's just in time for the evening poker game.

CHAPTER 44

The next afternoon, while Mom, Dad, Grandpa, and Grandma as are off playing golf, I wander down to the neighborhood recreation center. The rec. center houses a dozen or so bowling lanes, a pool hall, and a few shuffleboard courts. I slip through the door and into the air-conditioned building; lingering in the entryway for a moment and basking in the cool air.

I pass the empty shuffleboard courts first, walking toward the bowling lanes. Seven or eight of the lanes are full, and the strikes are rampant. These old guys are good. One old man catches my eye. He has a full head of snow-white hair and is frail, but strong somehow. When it's his turn he hobbles up to the line, the ball hanging limply from his arm. Then he pulls into his stance, his brow furrowed in concentration. With one swift, fluid motion he hurls the eighteen-pound orb down the lane and crashing into the pins, leaving none standing. With his task completed, he limps back to his seat. As the lane resets itself I turn around to see what's happening in the pool hall. The hall is the size of a basketball court, filled with dark green tables and low-slung lights. Most of the tables are empty, but a few of them are being circled by players, cues in hand.

"Damnit Clarence, concentrate!" the man closest to me mutters. I give him a sideways glance and realize that he's the only one at the table; he's talking to himself. I slide over a few steps and watch as a couple of men bang out a game of eight ball. Neither of them are doing very well; the man with Parkinson's Disease is having an especially difficult time. Soon tired of seeing them miss shots, I turn to get a better look at Clarence.

Like all of the other inhabitants of Sun City, Clarence is no young pup, but he's far from frail. Clarence is a large man, and he maneuvers with a surprising amount of grace; moving swiftly despite his obvious gut. From his mouth hangs a cigar, which he occasionally taps into an ashtray resting on the table. He is dressed in a well-worn white t-shirt and dark dress pants, making his tattered sandals look a bit out of place.

As I watch, Clarence proceeds to run the table. Starting with a vicious break, he starts to methodically drop balls in, not missing a single shot. Sometimes with a light tap, sometimes a sharp crack, he keeps at it until the table is nearly bare, leaving only the cue ball.

"Not bad, not bad," he mutters, then starts to pull to balls from their pockets to rack them. "Now is there anything I can help you with?" He continues to rack the balls, not looking up. "Kid, what do you want?" I look around, than wonder if he's talking to me.

"You mean me, sir?"

He looks up and frowns. "No, the other kid standing around watching me. Yes you!"

I take a step forward, "Nothing. I mean, I was just watching you play."

He adds a bit of chalk to his cue. "It's more of a performance when I play by myself. There's not really any competition." Another drag on the cigar. "What's you're name kid?"

"Will. Will Larkin."

He motions for me to come over. "Well, come here Mr. Larkin, maybe you can learn something." I walk over to the table, stopping just short of the bright circle of light that shines down upon it. "You ever play pool?" he asks.

I nod, "I play some, but not very often."

"You any good?"

"Not really."

He smiles, "Do you want do be?"

"Sure. What have you got?"

"All sorts of stuff. Here's something you can do to impress the ladies." Clarence selects six balls and drops the rest of them into the pockets. He then places one ball directly in front of each pocket. He sets the cue ball on one side of the table and lines up his shot. He turns to me and winks, and without looking back at the table he makes his shot. The cue ball careens off the bumper and smashes into each ball in turn. When the dust clears, only the cue ball remains.

"Wow," is my only reply.

He shrugs, "Set up shots are pretty easy, and they don't win you any games. What you need is the ability to work with what you're given." With that he racks the balls and places the cue ball, taking care to align it perfectly.

"Any tips for the break?" I ask.

"Use a fast, light cue, and don't be shy." He smashes the cue ball into the triangle, sending balls flying everywhere. "Pool is a fairly simple game," he says, pacing around the table and puffing on his cigar. "It's just a matter of angles and inertia. An excellent physics lesson really. Another ball is chipped into a side pocket. "Once you've got the basic shots down, it's mainly just a mental game."

"A mental game?" I echo.

He snaps another ball into a side pocket. "Once you know how you can make a shot, you should be able to make that shot every single time." He taps his forehead. "The only thing stopping you is your mind. It's not physical, it's not that you're not strong enough or fast enough. It's all in your head." He pauses, knocking the ash from his cigar. "I guess the same can be said for a lot of things." He snaps off another shot. "The shots themselves are all physics and geometry. If you can figure out where a ball will go when another ball hits it at a certain angle, the game gets a lot easier."

"How do you learn that?"

He shrugs. "Practice." Clarence checks the clock on the wall, "But anyway, don't you have to get back home for dinner?"

I look up at the wall and realize that I've been standing around the rec. center for over an hour. "I suppose so. Thanks for the lesson," I say, shaking his hand.

"It was a pleasure," he replies. With that he turns away, and goes back to concentrating on his game.

After dinner with the family I go out for an evening run. For the most part I'm not much of a runner, but when I'm here I start making exceptions. There's just something about the warm, soft, night air. Because it's a retirement community most of the streets are quiet at night, leaving the sidewalks and alleyways to me. I step out the front door, trot down the driveway, and turn onto the street, heading straight for the nearest golf course. I don't know what it is, but I've always liked the feeling of a golf course at night.

I slow down as I reach the edge of the course, looking around for anyone who might accuse me of trespassing. Finding no one, I slip onto the fairway. Without the sun the desert looses it's heat quickly, and the grass is already beaded with dew. I wander up and down the sculpted hills, drinking in the aroma of some unknown night flower. The stars are present, but nearly masked by the haze and the light of the city. As I pause to look at the stars, I hear something nearby; it's the sound of running water.

I work my way toward the sound, being careful not to plunge into a water hazard or some other unknown hole. Bit by bit, I realize where the pond is. The water reflects the streetlights, a liquid pool of blackness set in the grass. With the pond found, I still can't locate the source of the running water. Then I notice what looks like a hole in the surface of the water. The majority of the pond reflects the glare of the lights, but there is one circle in the center of the pond that is completely black. The black hole seems to be the source of the sound.

The inky abyss looks like the entrance to hell. It reflects no light, and offers no suggestion as to its purpose. Then it hits me. A drain! The little entrance to the center of the earth must be part of the watering system for the golf course. I sigh, somehow exhilarated by my newfound discovery. It's a little thing, sure, but I figured this out; it's my own little revelation. I jog home, my feet feeling a little lighter than before.

CHAPTER 45

*T*he next couple of days are spent in blissful relaxation. I end up spending an entire morning catching up on all of the homework I've been putting off. It's not as bad as it sounds though, since I finish the homework poolside at a nearby country club. Usually the ladies at any given pool would distract me from my studies, but here that isn't the case. On occasion I'll run into another kid who is visiting their grandparents as well, but the majority of the pool guests would qualify for The Sportsman's Café Senior Discount. My afternoon is an exciting mix of napping, finishing off my novel, and consuming unnatural amounts of Jones Soda.

During the afternoon, Grandma makes us a huge supper. She cooks a giant pot roast with mounds of mashed potatoes and gravy and steamed vegetables. For desert: peach cobbler. Bliss.

I spend my final morning in sunny Arizona out in the wilderness. Mom and I drive to the nearby White Tank Mountains, her to go running and me to go hiking. Mom usually takes her morning jog along the paths of Sun City, but sometimes she likes to try a little more scenic location.

Mom chooses a parking lot and we hop out. She jogs off down the road toward a nearby trailhead. I don't follow; instead I go off into the desert, starting up a nearby peak.

I would like to think that if I lived out here I would do this all the time. I love climbing, because it always seems to allow me to accomplish specific goals. When I'm climbing I know when I've succeeded and I know when I've failed. Two years ago Mom made me come down when I was nearly to the summit of a different mountain; I was furious. When we came back last year I made sure it was the first peak I climbed.

As I scramble toward my new goal I wonder if there are any rattlesnakes in the area. If I remember right, they're active year-round. I make a mental note to make sure I look before I put my hands or feet anywhere. Just then I feel a barrel cactus tear its way across my right calf, reminding me that snakes aren't the only things I have to worry about.

When I reach the first summit I enjoy a slight adrenaline rush; I made it. I pause for a moment and survey my surroundings. Behind me lies the Phoenix valley, its suburbs stretching to distant mountains, which I can hardly make out do to the haze. In front of me are more peaks, all covered with an assortment of cacti and shrubs. I decide to work my way along the ridgeline toward the next peak, just to see what I can see. As I pick my way along the ridge, taking care not to stumble over a rock and fling myself down the slope, I hear what sounds like a stream.

I pull myself onto a nearby boulder, trying to hear where it's coming from. It sounds like the sound is coming from a valley just over the next ridge. I still can't see the stream. I continue toward the noise, hopping over rocks and dodging cacti. As I reach the ridge and start down the other side I stop myself, ending about five feet from a shear cliff that drops off into the gorge below. I just stand there for a minute, trying to catch my breath. I then slowly approach the cliff and peer over the edge. It's about fifty of sixty feet to the valley below, and there is the stream. It's hard to tell how big it is from the ledge, but I can hear it clearly from my rocky perch.

I work my way along the ledge until I find a sloping crevasse about five feet wide. Moving along one wall to steady myself, I slowly work my way into the draw. The stream itself is about four feet wide, meandering around rocks and outcroppings, flowing swiftly in some places and collecting into deep pools in others. I start heading upstream. By hopping from rock to rock I stay fairly dry. Then I get to a shallow pool surrounded by cacti and thorned shrubs. Instead of looking for a way around it I go straight up the middle. That single hop gives me both wet shoes and an easier way to get upstream. Now instead of picking my way from rock to rock I can walk straight upstream. I go a bit higher when I reach another impasse. The stream drops from a ten or fifteen ledge into a deep pool, leaving me with a very pretty waterfall but no easy way to get around it. I decide against trying to climb the falls, scaling the slick rock would be suicidal, so I to look for a way around it. It only takes a second to find what I'm looking for, a thin trail cutting it's way up the outcropping. As I climb higher, the trail becomes thick with all sorts of plants that are trying to rip at my arms and legs, so I proceed slowly, trying to be as delicate as possible.

Halfway up I get sick of being attacked by every shrub I walk past, so I get it over with. I bull my way through the foliage, slashing up my flesh in the process. Once I reach the top of the ledge I find my way back to the creek and continue upstream. I come across another waterfall, this one only a foot or two high. I pause near it for a bit, just watching and listening as the water tumbles over the rocks. I check my watch and realize that the one-foot-falls will have to mark the extent of my exploration. It's time to head back.

I travel downstream in leaps and bounds, hopping and splashing from pool to pool, until I reach the waterfall. I don't want to go back down the path of pain very much. I wonder if I could just jump down. I creep closer to the edge, being careful not to slip on the wet rock. As I get closer I inch along on my back, with my arms beneath me and my legs out in front of me. I notice a smaller ledge farther down, and inch my way toward it.

It's hard to tell how far down the water is, but it must be at least ten or fifteen feet. The water below looks fairly dark and deep. Then again, that dark spot could very well be a rock instead of a deep hole. I look uphill, considering turning back, but then I realize it's out of the question. I had a hard time coming down the wet rock; there's no way I'll make it back up. There is still another crevasse in the rock a foot or two down, and I attempt to cram my feet into it, lowering myself that much closer to the water. Then I run out of ledges.

This is it. I look down, checking for the darkest spot in the pool (and hoping it isn't a rock). Then I take a deep breath and jump. For an instant I feel weightless, floating over the desert, and then the water screams up at me. I spread out as I hit the water, my arms and legs flailing in all directions. I instinctively pull for the surface and break through, gasping for air. Feeling the ground beneath my feet I stand up, the water coming up to my chest. Now certain that I am, in fact, alive, I turn to see where I had jumped from.

The cliff, now bespeckled with water from my plunge, towers above me. My heart pounding, I see that my final ledge looks to be about twelve feet from the water's surface. What a rush. I pull myself out of the pool, half swimming, half walking, and peel off my shirt. As I wring the water out of my t-shirt I wonder if anyone else has ever jumped from the same waterfall. I suppose it doesn't really matter; what does matter is that I did.

CHAPTER 46

I sigh as I settle into my seat on the plane, shoving my backpack under the seat in front of me. It was a good vacation, but it's time to go home. I look up in time to see my parents take their seats a few rows in front of me. Usually we're able to get three seats in the same row, but this time we're separated. Luckily I managed to get a window seat so I only have to be next to one stranger. I wonder who I'll get this time.

I flip through the plane's emergency pamphlet, wondering how all of the people can be so calm when performing a water landing at six hundred miles an hour, when I feel/hear someone sit down next to me. I look up, hardly believing my eyes: it's vintage leather jacket girl. This time she's wearing a faded denim jacket over a sky blue tank top and khakis. Her hair, now unhindered by any clips or bobby pins, frames her tanned face. She tosses her carry-on (a messenger bag) under the seat in front of her and drops into her seat.

My heart races. Here's my big chance. All of the stupid little inspirational sayings (seize the day)come flooding back to me (you only live once). I tap the safety pamphlet against my knee, wondering what I should do. Vintage leather jacket girl snickers, looking at the pamphlet.

"What a joke," she says.

I hesitate. "Excuse me?"

"All of this stuff about emergency landings," she replies, pointing at the manual. "Do you know how many successful water landings have been made by commercial airliners?" I shake my head. "Three. No one swam away from the rest of them."

"That's comforting," I say, shoving the pamphlet back in its pocket.

"Don't worry about it. You ever fly before? It's safer than driving."

"We fly down to see my grandparents every year. My name's Will, by the way." I extend my hand and she takes it.

"I'm Emily. My parents came down here on a business trip and offered to bring me with."

"Where'd you stay?"

"The Hilton in Phoenix, then we took a trip down to Mexico."

I sigh, "My dad and I took a road trip too, but I could have done without it."

"Why, what happened?"

"I just can't handled being trapped in a box with my dad for that long."

She laughs. "I know what you mean."

Then there is a lengthy pause as I frantically search for something else to say. To my horror, she pulls out a book! Must...save...conversation.

"What's the book?" I ask, making a swift recovery.

"To Kill a Mockingbird. I'm reading it for English."

"I remember reading it. I always thought Atticus was the coolest name in the world."

Her eyes open wide, "So did I! I'm definitely naming one of my kids Atticus."

I smile, "Me too." We let the idea hang for a minute, a twinge of tension looming in the air. A few images flash through my mind: a marriage, house and a white picket fence, little Atticus running around the yard.

"So William, what is it you do?" she asks.

"What do you mean?"

"Well, it seems to me that everyone has something they enjoy doing and that they do well. Sometimes it's something like running or baseball, or it can be talking to friends or reading books. So tell me, what do you do?"

I think for a second, considering the question. "Acting. I guess I'm an actor. What about you?"

"I'm a songwriter."

"Do you play guitar too?" I ask, hoping I don't sound like an idiot.

She smiles, "No, not yet. That's why I'm just a songwriter and not a full-blown musician. I've always wanted to play guitar, but I guess I've never gotten around to it."

"You should," I say, trying not to sound too enthused. A musician and a songwriter! More images flash by, hanging around our apartment helping her with lyrics, hearing her laugh, Atticus.

We talk music for twenty minutes or so; discussing bands, up-and-coming talent, concerts, lyrics, everything. She confides that though she's a diehard rock and ska fan, she still has a thing for the Backstreet Boys. In return I tell her that as a punk fan I still like some of my dad's oldies collection. She laughs.

"My God, I know! I love CCR, but I couldn't tell any of my friends at school. Not most of them at least, it'd ruin my image."

I scoff, "Your image?"

She shrugs, "Sure, everyone has a reputation to keep up, for better or for worse. What about you?"

I shake my head and laugh, "I guess I never thought about it that much. The reputation of a drama geek needs very little cultivating; it just sort of grows on it's own."

"Well…" she says, giving me a sly smile, "I don't know about the geek part."

We go on to talk about all sorts of things: books, movies, God knows what else. Nothing important I guess, but it's good nothings; it's fun. For the first time in my life I don't want the plane to land. I want the runway to be fogged over so we can fly in circles for hours. Despite my wishes, eventually we're on the ground. As everyone pries their bags and purses from the seats and compartments we scratch down our phone numbers and e-mail addresses, promising to call and write. As I walk down the jet way with my parents and leave Emily behind, I realize that I don't know if she has a boyfriend or not. Hell, I don't even know her last name.

CHAPTER 47

*A*s the saying goes, I like traveling, but I love coming home. Apart from meeting Emily, the best part of our homeward journey is walking in our front door. No place in the world smells like my house. For lack of a better term, it smells like home. It being late, I stumble downstairs and flop into bed.

Morning comes much too early. After I smack my alarm's snooze button a number of times I finally drag myself out of bed, only because the final time I hit the snooze button I knock the clock out of reach. I take my shower, turning the water to cold for the last ten seconds in an effort to wake myself up, but it's no use. This is a case for the Caffeine Gods.

On the way to school I stop by Common Grounds, the local coffee shop, and pick up a double depth charge. This dark concoction is a mix of one cup of the house blend with two shots of espresso. It sure beats the hell out of a cold shower. My caffeine fix secured, I go off in search of news.

"Hey Will, long time no see," Scott says as I walk into the lunch-room. I drop my bag and coffee next to him and stand in line for breakfast. Upon my return I ask for the report.

"So what have I missed? Just give me the headlines."

"Oh let's see…Our basketball team still sucks, no snow days, more busy work, I've got a date with Kate, Allison might be dating again, and there might be some trouble between Sara and Dave."

"All right, one at a time," I say, spreading cream cheese on my bagel, "What's going on with Sara and Dave?"

"I'm not sure exactly. There have been some rumors going around, and they're not as lovey-dovey as they usually are."

"And Kate?"

He smiles, "Yeah, I asked her out. We're going to have dinner on Friday."

"Congratulations. What about Allison?"

"I saw her with some guy at the basketball game last week. I'm not sure who it was, but they seemed pretty friendly."

"Wow, I guess I miss a lot if I'm gone for a week."

"It's a long time," he replies. "How was the trip?"

I thought the kid would never ask. I give him the highlights, especially my experience in cliff diving and my interactions with Emily.

"Are you going to call her?"

"I don't know. The last thing I need is another girl in my life."

"Come on, it sounds like you had a really good time with her."

"I did, but still, I don't want to get into a long distance relationship or anything, and I'm with Julie now. I don't even know where Emily lives."

"So what? No one said you have to be life partners or anything. Just be friends."

"I suppose that's not so bad. She was pretty cool to hang out with."

He smiles, "Well there ya go."

It doesn't take long to settle back into the routine of school. Julie is happy to see me and I pass Sara in the halls without incident. I'm curious about what's going on with her and Dave, but I figure I shouldn't be the one to ask. I could do without the cold weather, but other than that it's good to be back.

CHAPTER 48

I don't get back to the café until Thursday night. Apparently the café has undergone huge changes since I was gone, we have new steak knives. Since I've been here the only thing that's changed has been the open/closed sign on the door. The new knives are a nice feature, and unlike the old ones the blades don't fall out of them. I punch in, and only a few minutes later Cliff arrives.

"Willie!" he says, hobbling over to one of the counter stools. "Long time, no speekey. Where 'ya been?"

"I was down in sunny Arizona," I reply, pouring him a cup of coffee.

"Those poor girlies. What did they do without their Willie?"

I shrug, "I'm sure it was tough for them."

"What was it like when you got back?"

"I had to beat them off with a stick."

He smiles, "Yeah, I know what that's like."

The majority of the night goes well. The regulars come in as always, and they're eager to hear of my travels. I tell them about cliff diving, swimming, and sunshine, but decide to leave out the part about Emily. The waiter/customer relationship is an odd one n the café. I am their waiter, their friend, and a relay of the day's current events. The duties overlap from time to time, and sometimes the lines between them become a bit blurry. In this respect I'm happy to tell them about the trip, but I don't hesitate to leave certain things out.

Around 7:30 I start to slow down. I've gotten fairly used to it by now; after a whole day of school and a few hours at the café I start to get worn out. Around 8, when I'm starting to clean things up and get stuff set out for the morning wait staff, two strangers walk in. Even if someone's not a regular I've usually seen them before. These two are unfamiliar.

Walking through the front door are two scraggly looking guys, mid 30s, wearing stained flannel shirts and torn jeans. One of them stumbles as he gets through the door and steadies himself on the other. Eventually they sit down, choosing a booth in the middle of the restaurant. Things don't seem right, but regardless of what I think, I don't have much choice in the matter. I sent the other waitress home early since we were so slow, so now I have to serve them. I fill two glasses with water, grab a pot of coffee, and walk over to their table.

"Hi there," I say, setting down the water, "Do either of you want a cup of coffee?"

"I'll take a cup," one of them says, flipping over a coffee cup on the table, "How about you Lenny?" The other man, Lenny, doesn't reply. He just stares out the window, watching cars go by. "Lenny! You want coffee?" Lenny snaps to, looking at me for the first time.

"Ah, no, I don't want no coffee. It burns me, 'member?"

I nod and pour the first man coffee. "You guys need a minute to order?"

The first man grabs two menus, shoving one into Lenny's hands. "Yeah, we'll need a second."

I return to the counter, putting the coffee pot back on the burner. "Anybody know those guys?" I ask the crew at the counter. Three heads swivel to check out the interlopers, then turn back.

"I've never seen 'em before," Ken replies, stirring some cream into his coffee. The other guys both shrug. I go about my closing duties, covering the pies and rolls with Saran Wrap, but keep an eye at the two new guys. After a few minutes I go back to take their orders.

Lenny has gone back to watching cars go by, but the first man sees me as I approach. He smiles, displaying a jagged row of yellow teeth. When I get to the table I notice a new smell hanging in the air: alcohol. It's tough to say for sure which of the two has been drinking, but the smart money is on the second man.

"I think we know what we want," he says, opening a menu. "I'll have a half-pound burger with onion rings and mozzarella sticks, and Lenny here'll have four pieces of French toast, woncha' Lenny? Lenny!" Once again, Lenny tears his gaze from the road and looks around.

"French toast is here Jeff?"

Jeff shakes his head, "No, but you like French toast, don't ya?" Lenny nods. "And get him a chocolate milk to drink." Lenny's eyes light up.

"Chocolate milk?! I love chocolate milk!"

Jeff nods, "That's nice Len. That should be about it. And hurry it up, would ya? We're in a rush."

I go back to the kitchen window to put in the order and Lenny gets up and heads toward the bathroom. I'm getting Lenny's milk when I hear the scream.

"Jeff!! Help Jeff!" I spin around to look at the door of the bathroom, expecting water to come gushing out or to see Lenny stagger out with a severed arm. Jeff runs inside to help with whatever the problem is. A few minutes later Jeff comes out, infuriated.

"You don't have any paper towels in the bathroom." He screams, pointing at me.

I shrug, "It might have run out. Do you want some napkins or something?"

"You don't understand, we need towels."

"I don't get it, why can't you just use a napkin?"

"My brother's wife left him today and he's had a couple drinks. Lenny's a little slow, and he don't like change much, but when he's drinking he can't handle it when things aren't the way they should be. Now can you find us any towels?"

"I'll check," I say, walking back to the dry storage room. Nothing. "Sorry," I say, walking back to the front. "No luck."

He shakes his head, "This isn't good." With that he goes back to the bathroom to help Lenny.

I yell back to the kitchen, "Mark, I might need some help out here." Mark walks out to the front, wiping his hands on his shirt.

"What's going on?" he asks.

"The two guys that came in a little while ago, one of 'em has been drinking and right now he's not very happy."

"Why, what happened?"

"We don't have any paper towels." He shoots me a quizzical glance. "Don't ask." A high wailing comes from the men's room, followed by a loud crash.

"Call the cops," Mark says.

"What?!"

"Call the cops now."

"Why would I want to call the-" But mark ignores me, going to the phone himself. I follow. "Why do you need the cops?"

He dials the phone, "I had a cousin who drank like that. When he got angry he'd just rage. Trust me."

Another wail comes from the restroom. Jeff flies out of the door and smashes up against the wall. He looks around, mumbles an apology, and goes back in. I look around the café, and every head is turned in the direction of the bathroom. We hear another crash, followed by Jeff yelling something. It feels like it takes forever before the cops arrive. A few minutes later the two squad cars pull up within twenty seconds of each other and the officers come in together.

"Where is he?" the tall one asks. I point to the restrooms. As they approach the bathroom door he calls out, "Lenny? We're coming in now, take it easy." With their hands on their belts the officers walk into the restroom. As the entire café listens we hear some low talking followed by a shout: Lenny. Then there is a quick scuffle, and all is quiet. A few moments later all four men emerge. Lenny is in handcuffs, being led by the police officers, and Jeff following close behind.

"I guess you can cancel our orders," Jeff says to Mark as he walks by. The shorter of the two officers nods to me.

"Sorry for the trouble," he says, and with that they're gone.

Lenny becomes the talk of the café for the evening, with all of the old guys at the counter chattering about it. As a result, they all end up staying later than usual. Despite me locking the door and tossing around the keys, some of the patrons stay until almost ten. I'm about to shove a coffee pot down everyone's throat by the time they finally leave. When I get home I still have a paper to finish for English, and I don't get to bed until after midnight.

Maybe it's the late night and the lack of sleep. It could also be the drunken yelling or the coffee-drinking leeches, but not matter what the cause, I get out of bed grumpy.

CHAPTER 49

$\mathcal{I}$f I make it through today I can finally enjoy my weekend, but the fact isn't very heartening. I grumble a hello at my parents as I go out the door, not wanting to talk to anyone. In this mood, Julie is not well received.

"Willie!" she says, jumping up from her seat at the school breakfast table. I hate it when she calls me that. "I missed you," she says, smiling. She runs up to me and gives me a big kiss, with a little covert tongue action thrown in for good measure. I push her away. "What's wrong?" she asks.

"Nothing," I reply, shrugging her off.

"Aww, is my Willie grumpy?"

"Don't call me Willie."

"Come on," she says, hitting my shoulder, "You know you like it."

I reply coldly. "I don't, actually. There are a lot of things you don't know about me."

"Aww, you're not kidding anybody. You like it, my little Willie."

My jaw clenches involuntarily, "Actually, I am not your little Willie, not anymore."

"What do you mean?" she asks, cocking her head.

I take a deep breath, "I mean that 'we' are no more. I'm happy to be your friend, but us being a couple just isn't working out."

She falters a bit, taken aback. "What do you mean? We're doing fine."

"Julie, we are not fine. We never were. This whole thing was a bad idea from the start."

She stares at me for a moment, saying nothing. Tears begin to well up in her eyes and she turns away, running for the women's bathrooms. I continue walking down the hallway, getting sideways glances from the people I pass. I seem to be getting a lot of that lately. I feel bad about hurting her feelings, really I do. I'm also somewhat surprised I ended it. I usually plan this sort of thing. I suppose it's for the better. It was going to end eventually, and I suppose sooner is better, less painful. It's better, I'm sure.

I spend the majority of the next 24 hours pondering my current predicament. I see Julie in the halls once or twice and she passes without a word. If I had to guess, I'd say the chances of a friendship are about nil, but it's not a huge loss. On Friday I decide to herd up to the crew and head for the movies.

CHAPTER 50

I meet Allison, Aaron, Richard, and Bish at the movie theatre. We could have gone to the multiplexes in Elk River or St. Cloud, but we opt for the good 'ol Milaca Theatre. It has more character.

We meet just inside the door, out of the cold, before we go in. We each pay our whopping $2.50 for tickets, get a couple buckets of popcorn for the five of us, and go inside. As we try to find our seats I notice Julie sitting down. She's cuddling with some new guy. I guess it didn't take her very long to move on.

We settle into our seats and wait for the previews to start, staring at a blank screen and listening to country music. As Allison and I share a tub of popcorn, I consider asking her my question.

"Hey Al," I say, digging for another handful of popcorn, "You ever think about what it'd be like if we dated?"

"Weird," she says, not missing a beat. I think for a second, trying to decide if that's good or bad. "We're such good friends now," she continues, "It'd just be strange."

"Wait a minute," I reply, "What's with all this 'now' talk? Are you saying that there was a then?"

"Of course. I had a huge crush on you for like six months."

"What? When was this?"

"Ninth grade, when we sat next to each other in geometry."

"Huh," I say, turning a piece of popcorn over in my hand, "I had no idea."

She shrugs, "That's men for ya." My brow furrows; another ambiguous comment. "Hey, isn't that Sara?" she says, pointing toward the front of the theatre. There, a few rows in front of us, are Sara and Dave.

"Yes, that's them," I mumble, turning my attention back to the popcorn.

She smiles, "You could go and say hi, 'ya know."

I try to scowl, but break into a smile. "Shaddup." The lights start to go down. "You know, I had a crush on you once."

"Really?" she asks, turning toward me. "When?"

"The beginning of freshmen year, before we had geometry together. I wrote all kinds of notes that I never gave you." I shake my head, "It's weird to think how different things could have been."

"Hey! We're trying to watch a movie," someone behind us hisses. I look up and realize that the show has started, effectively ending our trip down memory lane.

Throughout the movie I pay very little attention to the film itself. Most of my time is divided between talking to Al, throwing food at Aaron, and keeping an eye on Dave and Sara. About halfway through the movie, right after Tom Hanks meets Meg Ryan for dinner, Sara screams.

"What the hell do you think you're doing?!" she yells, standing up.

"No, Sara, come back," Dave says in a harsh whisper. She ignores him. When she makes it to the aisle she goes straight for the door. Dave, close behind, stumbles over a few people before he too reaches the aisle and follows behind her. I look at the door, then to the screen, and back to the door.

"Go," Allison says, nudging me in the ribs. "Don't miss your chance this time." Al's right. She usually is. I get up, nodding to Aaron, Richard, and Bish.

Aaron whispers, "Go get her," as I walk by, and I smile in appreciation. I move toward the front door slowly, not wanting to walk into the middle of anything, but not wanting to miss anything either. I can see them outside as I reach the entrance. Dave has finally caught up with her. Dave says something, probably pleading with her, but then she turns away. Dave watchers her go, then starts to walk back inside.

I spin around, looking for a place to hide. Jumping in front of the candy counter, I pretend to be considering my choices as he walks by. Once Dave passes I run out the door, hoping to find Sara. When I get out on the sidewalk I take a look around, but I can't see her. Etiquette would say that she came here in Dave's car, and since he's still inside with the keys she couldn't have gone very far. The park. I'll bet she went to the park.

I jog the two blocks to the city park, checking every street and alley as I pass. She's there, sitting on a park bench in a pool of amber light, staring into a puddle of melted snow. She might be crying, but it's hard to tell from where I'm standing. For an instant I consider turning back; forgetting Sara altogether and chasing after Emily or Allison or someone, but then the instant passes. I walk slowly, dragging my feet so she can hear me approach. She looks up once, then turns away.

"It's a nice night," I say, stopping near the bench.

"Depends on how you look at it," she replies, looking at the sky. This may make or break my entire relationship with Sara. I've got to find a way to cheer her up. Jokes.

"What has two legs and bleeds?" I ask.

She glares at me," If you say anything about girls I will seriously kill you."

"It's not that," I say, shaking my head.

"I don't know then," she replies, "What?"

"Half a dog." She doesn't laugh. Damnit.

"That's pretty sick," she says. I shrug, defeated. "And for what it's worth, you really suck at cheering people up."

"Who's trying to cheer anyone up?" I reply indignantly. "I was just out for a little walk."

"In the middle of a movie?"

"It wasn't that great anyway. And it *is* a beautiful night."

"Well, if you don't mind, I'd really like to be alone right now," she says, looking back to her reflection in the puddle.

"You sure you don't want to talk about it?"

She nods, "I'm sure."

I shrug, "OK, but if you want to talk, just let me know."

"Thanks."

"And take a look around," I say, "It really is a nice night." I turn back toward the theatre and walk away. When I get back, Dave is nowhere to be found. I find my seat in the theatre, stumbling over Allison as I sit down. To the disgust of the lady behind me, I tell her everything that happened.

"Will," she says after I finish, "You did the right thing." That night I sleep the unobstructed sleep usually reserved for infants and puppies.

CHAPTER 51

*T*he following Monday I make it a point to talk to Ann Meier, Sara's best friend. I find her in the commons before school and pull her aside.

"Ann, you've got to help me with something."

"What is it?"

"I was talking to Sara on Friday night and she was really upset. I want to know what happened."

"It's personal," she replies.

"Listen, I know it was something that Dave did, I just want to find out what. I want to help."

"No."

"Ann, really, I want to help Sara out."

She sighs, "Ok, but you can't tell anyone else. I shouldn't even be telling you, but Dave tried to put the moves on her and he went too far." She pauses. "Don't try to get too deep into this one Will, she's kind of anti-male right now."

"I'll bet. Thanks Ann."

"No problem."

That bastard. I knew it; I knew he'd hurt her. Brief visions of beating him within an inch of his life flash through my mind. Then again, it really isn't any of my business. I can't run around beating up every guy who tries to go too far with a girl. But this is Sara. This is different. I chuckle in spite of myself. I can see the headlines now: "William the Righteous, Defender of Freedom." Right.

CHAPTER 52

"Mister Williams!" I yell across the parking lot. "Can I have a word with you?" Dave looks up as he unlocks his car door. "What do you want?"

I stop just short of his trunk, "I hate to say I told you so, but I told you so."

He scowls, "What are you talking about?"

"Sara. You just had to go too far with her, didn't you?"

He takes a step toward me, "I thought I told you to stay out of it."

"I'm not a part of anything," I argue, "I'm just an observer."

"Bullshit. What did you say to her?"

I shrug. "Nothing. I was just trying to comfort the poor girl."

"You'd better stay the hell away from Sara."

"I'm sorry Davey, but you don't control her life. Actually, you probably won't even be her boyfriend much longer."

He gives out a short, harsh laugh. "That's what you think. Little Sara is just a bit unsure of what she wants, but she'll figure things out soon enough." He grins. "I know she wants it."

I take a few steps closer and then, without thinking, I hit him. He falters a bit, probably due as much to the surprise as to the actual impact. I'm surprised myself, and I stare at my own fist in amazement. What did I just do?

"You're going to regret that," he says, touching his hand to his lip. He rushes at me, throwing me into the side of a nearby van. I try to push him off, but he's throwing punches indiscriminately, none of them landing square.

"Knock it off!" yells someone to my left. Huge arms intervene, pulling us apart. "What do you guys think you're doing?" I look up and realize the voice belongs to Tony Dickerson, our school's police liaison officer.

Ten minutes later I'm sitting in the assistant principal's office.

"William, I have to say I'm quite disappointed," Mr. Johnson says. "What was this all about?"

"Nothing," I reply.

"Don't waste my time. Guy's don't loosen each other's teeth over nothing. What was it?"

I sigh, "Girls. Well, a girl, more specifically."

"I should have figured. Now, you threw the first punch, right?"

I nod, "He was insulting Sa-, a friend of mine."

"Ah ha. So it was an act of chivalry?"

"I suppose."

"Listen Will, usually we send you home for three days if there's any fighting, that's the standard. But in this case you're both in good standing regarding both academics and behavior, and it sounds like this was a one-time occurrence. It better stay a one time occurrence, understand?" I nod again. This isn't going so bad after all. "I don't want to mar your record for something like this, so in this case I've decided to give you both a full day of detention, and I'll be sending a letter home to your parents. Does that make sense?"

"Yes. Thank you Mr. Johnson."

"Now don't let it happen again. And close your door on your way out." With that I am free to go. I walk out of his office and go to the commons, still in a state of semi-shock. I sigh. All and all I feel pretty good about the whole thing. Things could have gone a lot worse. It's hard to believe I finally did it; I finally gave him a little of what he deserves. Bastard.

I walk over to the men's bathroom and check myself out in the mirror. There's a slight bruise on my left cheek. Pulling up my shirt I notice a couple light bruises on my stomach, but my jacket seemed to take most of the abuse. Overall, there are no major injuries and no blood whatsoever. Not bad.

When I get home my parents don't find out about any of it. My story is that the bruise is from walking into a door; a humiliating story, but a plausible one. Lying to them is an obvious risk; if they read about this in the letter before they hear it from me things will be much worse, but I'm willing to take my chances. If things go well they'll never even see the letter.

CHAPTER 53

I end up working the following Wednesday. It's a slow night, and I don't even have any homework to finish due to my entire day of detention. It wasn't all that bad I guess; I managed to get ahead in all my classes and I even studied for my chemistry test. I managed to intercept the parent letter, so that's taken care of. There's even an added bonus. Since I wasn't suspended, none of this will go on my permanent record.

The weather has turned sour by the time I get off work; a freezing rain begins to coat everything with a thin layer of ice. Wonderful. My tires spin as I pull out of the parking lot, reminding me that traction isn't always a given. When I'm about halfway home, I don't realize what's going on until it's too late.

The car in front of me, a red Plymouth minivan, is stopped in my lane, getting ready to make a left hand turn. I apply the brakes slowly, not wanting to slide on the slick road. It takes me a second or two to realize that I'm not slowing down. I try to swerve out of the way. My wheels turn, but the car doesn't. Neither does the minivan. A second or so before the actual impact, everything seems to slow down.

My car piles into the van, almost without a sound. Everything seems to be frighteningly clear as the hood of my car crumples and buckles. I am thrown against my seat belt, only to be flung back into my seat. The van, it's rear end smashed, skids into the opposite lane, only to be nailed by an oncoming truck. It spins into the ditch, and the truck slides to a stop. Then everything is still.

I sit behind the wheel for a moment, feeling the adrenaline rush through my body and trying to understand what just happened. Another car arrives and stops along the shoulder of the road.

"Are you ok?" the man yells, climbing out of his car. I don't move. "Hey!" he says, opening my passenger side door, "You ok?"

"Yeah, I'm fine," I manage to reply. I look around. The minivan and the truck are both along the far shoulder; steam rises up from the hood of the mangled truck. What have I done? I try to open my driver's side door but it's jammed; I'm forced to climb out the passenger's side.

It's still raining. An ugly, freezing drizzle taps against the smashed vehicles. A few more cars have stopped, their occupants helping with the other victims or directing traffic around the scene of the accident. Two guys manage to climb out of the truck, crawling through the back window of the cab. No one has come out of the van yet.

It isn't long before the first squad car arrives. Since both my car and the green Ford pickup are now empty, he rushes over to the minivan. Suspended in disbelief, I stand by the side of the road and watch. Jumbled noises drift from the direction of the van; it doesn't sound good. Another police officer arrives shortly, splaying more red light across the icy road. Now begins the questioning.

I try to ignore the red van and focus on the occupants of the other truck, Pete and Derek, as they are questioned. I catch only bits and pieces of the conversation, noting that they are construction workers on their way home from St. Cloud, and that it seemed like the van just jumped out in front of them. Then they point at me.

The ambulance arrives, a howling tangle of red and white lights flying in from the darkness. I watch in horror as the occupants of the van, a woman and a small boy, are carried out on stretchers. I think I'm going to be sick. I steady myself against a nearby car; making an effort to keep myself from throwing up.

"Excuse me sir," a voice says. I look up to see a police officer standing over me. "Have you seen the driver of this vehicle?" He points at my car.

I nod. "Yeah, it was me. I was driving."

"Are you ok?" he asks.

Another nod, "I'm fine."

"We should probably get you checked out," he says, starting to lead me toward the ambulance. I stop.

"No. Not now at least. They have more important things to worry about. Do you need to take a statement or something?"

He shrugs, "Just a couple notes." He pulls out a pen and a pad. "What happened?"

I speak in fragments, "I was driving, icy road, and she stopped. She was turning left. I hit the brakes, nothing happened. Tried to swerve, and the car wouldn't turn. Just slid. Then I hit her."

He nods, then flips his pad shut, "I guess that will do for now."

"I should probably call my parents."

"You should, but not quite yet. Let's get you looked at first. The officer takes me over to a second ambulance that arrived during our chat.

Later on, all of the logistics of a car crash are taken care of. Everything that must be done is done, the exchanging of insurance information, the physical checkup, the choking, blubbering explanation to my parents; all is done in due time. When I finally get home I am exhausted, and I head for my bedroom the minute I get in the door. I suppose it's for the best. I don't want to talk to my parents about this any more than I already have; not yet at least.

CHAPTER 54

*T*he next morning I am forced to ride into town with my dad, and that means I'm also forced to talk to him. To get it out of the way, I begin my tale as soon as he starts the engine. Knowing I have nothing else to lose, I give him the unedited version. He listens without comment; allowing me to finish before he speaks.

"It sounds like you screwed up, huh?" I nod. "So now what are we going to do about it?" I shrug, not wanting to dig myself a hole I can't get out of. "It sounds like your car might be totaled, and you were at fault so you won't get much money from any insurance companies. Where does the money come from?"

"My savings, I suppose."

"Do you know how much this is going to cost?"

I shrug, "Not really, but whatever I can't pay for now I can work off."

"That's good," he replies, adjusting in his seat. "I don't mean to lecture you, but what have I always told you about driving?"

"Anticipation is the most important part of driving," I grumble.

"That's right. And when the roads are that icy a little anticipation goes a long way." I don't reply. Honestly, I don't really need this right now. I think I've gone through enough in the past 24 hours, thank you very much. Of course, I don't tell him any of this. For a high school junior, the only thing worse than riding to school with your dad is riding to school on the bus.

When he finally dumps me off at school I feel a little twinge in my lower back. I guess I didn't escape completely unscathed after all.

I am forced to field questions all morning. What happened? Where was the accident? Was anybody hurt? I repeat my answers again and again. I give most of them just enough information to shut them up, but I give a few friends the entire story. Most are sympathetic, but of course a select few have to be dicks and blame everything on me. I'll admit, a lot of it was my fault, but this really isn't the time to bring it up. Maybe some other time, when my car and spine are both functioning properly, but not now.

"Will, how are you? I heard about what happened; how are you doing?" It's Sara.

"Ah, not too bad," I reply. I look around; no Dave. "I don't know about the others though."

"I thought you were alone."

"I was, I mean the people in the other cars. Two of them were fine, but the other two had to be taken to the hospital."

"Do you know how they're doing now?"

"No, I'm not sure what their names are, so I don't know how I would find out. I feel terrible though. They didn't do anything wrong." Now that I've said it, I do feel kind of bad. At first I was just looking for some pity with that comment, but it's there. I suck.

"But the roads were really icy last night; it wasn't all your fault."

I sigh. "I suppose you're right."

"Anyway," she says, looking over her shoulder, "I guess I should get to class. I'll talk to you later."

"I'll be looking forward to it," I reply. Wow. She talked to me. See that? No move on my part whatsoever. She just walked right up and talked to me. No yelling, no scolding me for attacking her boyfriend, just talking. Interesting.

Later in the day I probe my usual gossip sources for information. It sounds like Sara and Dave haven't broken up or anything, but things have grown fairly cold. The end may be near.

CHAPTER 55

*T*he day after, Friday, Dad and I leave for Grandma's after school. It's a beautiful day. The snow is melting along the sides of the road; leaving a black, gritty residue of gravel and salt. The trees are just starting to bud, the leaves pushing their way free from their casings. I'm content just to ride along and watching spring unfold. I'm not that lucky.

"Now, don't forget," Dad says, "This car is not a gift. Since the Oldsmobile is totaled we needed to find you something else, but it had to be cheap. Your grandma agreed to lend you her car. In payment, you get to do chores." This is all new to me.

"Chores? What kind of chores?"

"Farm work. In return for the car you'll be helping your Uncle Tim on his farm for a few weeks this summer."

"A few weeks!? What about my vacation?"

He becomes stern. "You can't afford your own car, nor could you if you waited tables for three weeks. This little arrangement allows you to pay off your current debts without creating new ones. You are getting a deal."

I try to summon up a reply, but nothing comes. I'm sure I'll think of something in a few hours. I'll be lying in bed and come up with some scathing remark that would send him reeling. I hate it when that happens.

"And be careful with this one," he adds, "Cars aren't' supposed to be disposable." I don't give him the satisfaction of a reply.

The car itself is a bit different from what I'm used to. Being accustomed to the four cylinder Olds, the huge Buick Electra 225 looks like an aircraft carrier. A relic from the late 70's, it's commonly known as the "duce and a quarter;" the beast could probably weigh two and a half tons. Simply put, the thing is a boat. I don't know how I'll manage to pilot the hulk of green metal into a parking space.

"Your grandma said it uses quite a bit of oil, so you'll have to check it every time you put gas in it." He chuckles. "It might get twelve miles to the gallon on a good day, so you'll be putting in gas pretty often." Great.

I fire up the Buick for the first time, preparing to follow my dad back home. A thick blue cloud of smoke boils from the rear of the car, rolling over itself again and again. Wonderful. Just wonderful. When I finally get the beast hauling down the road it does, in fact, drive like a boat. With so much mass it seems to float down the road; or maybe "plow through" would be a better term. It makes big, slow, sweeping turns. Actually, everything seems slowed down. Acceleration, braking, speed, all of it seems slower. It's strange to look around the inside of a vehicle and see all of this empty space. It's like driving a gymnasium. I spend part of the ride home changing all of the radio presets; the original ones are all set to either gospel or classical stations. It looks like the radio has become my new friend; the Buick is without a tape or CD player. It just has the good 'ol AM/FM to keep me company. On the bright side, it's better than listening to Dad for another hour.

CHAPTER 56

One benefit of the Buick: I can fit my entire mountain bike in the trunk just by taking off the front wheel. Today is the first Saturday in a long time that I haven't had to work, so I'm taking full advantage of it. Aaron and I decided to go mountain biking for the day. Surprisingly, Milaca has one of the best trail systems in the state. We've decided to start early this year, getting in some training before the first races of the season. The snow has been melting fast this past week, and the trails themselves should be clear.

We meet at the trailhead at 10:00. Aaron is already there as I wheel the Buick into the little parking lot. I hop out and walk around to open the trunk.

"Whoa," Aaron says, riding circles around the car. "Nice ride."

"Shut up, it moves. That's enough."

"It's like, ten times bigger than your old car. How many people can you fit in it?"

"Six legally," I reply, "Probably twice that if you're not too picky about seat belts." I finish with my front tire. "You ready to go?"

"Sure. Where do you want to go first?"

I shrug. "Let's do the whole thing. It's been awhile since we've ridden the entire course." He nods, and we head off.

Oddly enough, Aaron and I are fairly well matched riding partners. Aaron, with his runner's build and small stature, excels at climbing. I, on the other hand, have a bit more ballast and tend to make up for lost time on the downhills. Inertia and gravity are my friends. Since we're pretty much even on the flats, we end up being relatively equal.

I acknowledge the importance of regular exercise within the first mile. A winter of play practice and waiting tables does very little to help my fitness level. The fact that much of the trail is covered with thick black mud doesn't help the situation, and by the second mile it feels like I'm going to blow my lungs out of my nose.

"Maybe we should take a break for a minute," Aaron says, huffing. I nod in agreement and we stop at the top of a slight rise. I pull out my water bottle and take a few big gulps. Much better.

"What do you think of the trail?" I ask.

"It's really soft, but it looks like it's in decent shape."

"Unlike myself," I add.

Adam chuckles, "What do you mean? Round is a shape."

"Shut up."

"Hey, by the way, I heard you and Sara are still talking."

"Yeah. Why wouldn't we be?"

"Well, I just figured she might be a little angry; since you punched her boyfriend and everything."

I shrug. "I guess not. Then again, it doesn't sound like they're on the best of terms either."

"Nice. Come to think of it, I heard he was hitting on Kate Basset the other night," Adam adds.

"Figures. God he's pathetic. Did anything come of it?"

"Of course not. She's got a boyfriend."

"What? Who?"

"Some guy from Minneapolis. You didn't know?"

"I had no idea. I guess neither did Scott."

"What do you mean?" he asks.

"Scott was kind of eying her, but I guess he didn't make his move soon enough."

"Huh. That's too bad."

"He'll get over it. Ready to go?" He nods. "Then let's go."

We drop off down the ridge, dodging pines and aspens. The ride feels cleansing somehow; working the winter blah out of my muscles. Aaron and I banter back and forth for the duration, flinging insults back and forth between us.

"Get up the hill fatty fatty fat fat."

"I'll break you in half, twig boy."

It happens every time we go out, and we've both accepted it as something that is done.

"You climb like a rhinoceros."

"Do you kiss your mother with that mouth, monkey boy?"

We insult each other on the trail, and then once we're off the trail all is forgotten.

CHAPTER 57

*M*onday morning's chemistry class is even more exciting than our ride. I run into Sara's friend Ann first, and decide to tell her about Dave.

"Did you hear about Evil Dave?" I ask, dropping my books off at my desk.

She sighs, "What is it this time?"

"He was hitting on Kate Basset."

"And?"

"She shot him down, but isn't he supposed to be with Sara?"

"I doubt it. Not for long anyway. And stop that."

"Stop what? I'm not doing anything."

"Look Will, I know your intentions are good, but don't go jumping all over Sara. She needs a break for a little while, ok?" I nod. "I mean, I think it's good that you like Sara, she could do a lot worse, but she's going to need some time."

"All right. Thanks Ann."

"No problem," she replies.

So she could do worse, huh? It sounds like I actually have a chance. Nice. The odds just nudged up a couple points. I see Scott come in the room and think back to the ordeal with Kate. I guess I'll have to break the news sooner or later. I sigh. Might as well be sooner.

"Hey Scott," I say, calling to him from across the room. He walks over.

"What?"

"I've got some news for ya. Evil Dave is up to his old tricks."

"What did he do this time?"

"He was hitting on Kate."

"Christ," he says, "She's not going out with him, is she?"

"Nope. Apparently she's dating some guy from Minneapolis."

"When did that happen?"

"A few months ago. I guess it's pretty serious."

Scott shakes his head. "I suppose that changes our odds some."

"I'll give you ninety to ten against."

He sighs, "And so begins a new chase."

"Anybody in mind?"

He shakes his head. "Maybe I should diversify and try to find some new markets."

"Other schools?"

"Yeah, but how?"

"What about basketball games?" I ask. "You could cruise our opponents' stands."

"Not a bad idea," he says. The bell rings and we all wander to our seats.

"All right everybody," Ms. Jamison says, "Today I have a demonstration for you dealing with the reactivity of different elements. As we've talked about, usually the higher series numbers will be the most reactive. In this jar I have a piece of sodium," she says, pulling out a small container. "Sodium reacts violently with water, so it is kept in a solution of alcohol to keep it from reacting with the moisture in the air." She puts on a pair of gloves and opens the jar. "I'm going to cut a piece of it off and immerse it in water. The result should be quite enlightening." She pulls out a small paring knife and begins to cut the fist-sized chunk of material. Things are going fine, until the knife slips.

The blade catches on Ms. Jamison's glove, and as she pulls her hand away she hits the block of sodium, sending it flying. The chunk lands in our scrub sink, where we wash our beakers and test tubes. Unfortunately, it's filled with water. The sink erupts with a thundering report, spewing water and shards of glass across the front of the classroom. The sodium hisses and sparks in the sink for a bit, then finally settles down. No one speaks. I look around and realize that Ms. Jamison is nowhere to be found. Then I see her, peeking her head up from behind her desk.

"Is everyone ok?" she asks. A few students answer with a soft "Yes." She walks over to the sink and peers in. "That was a little larger of a sample than I had planned for." The sink is destroyed, all of the fixtures bent, the enamel scorched. The desk, too, is a mess. All of the papers and books on it are soaked, and most of them covered with bits of shattered glass. Jamison picks up a soaked pile of papers and brushes away the glass. "These are the quizzes from last week," she says, dropping them back on the table. "They weren't in the grade book, so those of you who did poorly, be glad that sodium reacts violently with water." A few knowing nods are passed back and forth among the class.

Placed up against the explosion, the notes we take for the rest of the hour seem unbelievably dull.

CHAPTER 58

I guess it's true, the idea that if you put things off they tend to catch up with you. I have a large social project due on Wednesday regarding The Bill of Rights. I, being engrossed with important stuff like mountain biking, let it slip my mind. Today is Tuesday, and I am in trouble.

I spend the majority of my afternoon in the media center, digging up different examples of case law and hunting down the history of the different amendments. There are a few like myself scattered about, copying pages from encyclopedias or browsing the 'net, but not many. At this point most have either finished the project or have given up altogether.

By the time the library closes, I loathe The Bill of Rights. I hate them with all of my being. I would be perfectly content if the founding fathers would have never created them. Go ahead, read my mail, force me to be Protestant, censor the media, just don't make me do this paper.

I eat dinner in a huff; speaking only when spoken to. Shortly thereafter I'm back at my computer, dredging through loads of useless information to find what I need. A few hours later, finished with most of the raw information gathering, I start on the actual paper. About halfway through I remember another overlooked detail: the collage.

I check my assignment sheet, hoping my memory is mistaken. No such luck. In addition to our five-page paper, we are also required to put together a collage representing the things that the Bill of Rights protects. Where the hell am I supposed to find pictures for a collage? We get magazines like Bicycling and Better Homes and Gardens, where am I going to get an image for double jeopardy? Maybe Scott knows.

I dial his number, knowing it by heart. No answer. I decide to try Sara instead. I remember her number too, having engraved it in my memory a few months ago.

"Hello?" a female voice says.

"Hi. Is Sara there?"

"This is."

"Hey Sara, it's Will. I was wondering, have you finished your project for social yet?"

"Yeah, haven't you?"

"Ah, not quite. I was wondering, how did you manage to find pictures for your collage?"

"I cut most of them from magazines. Why?"

"I can't find anything on double jeopardy or the garrison of troops. There just aren't many courtroom scenes in Better Homes and Gardens."

"I had that problem too," she says. "I found most of the court stuff online and then just printed the pictures."

"That's not a bad idea," I seriously should have thought of that myself.

"I really should add more to mine, but I think I'm just going to go to bed," she says.

"Long day?"

"You have no idea."

"What happened?"

"I'm just realizing how stupid I've been," she says.

"Dave?"

"Yeah."

"Why, did you break up with him?" I ask the question with care, trying to avoid any land mines that I might stumble upon.

"Yeah, something I should have done a long time ago. But anyway, good luck on the project, I'm going to bed."

"Goodnight Sara."

"Bye."

I love the Bill of Rights.

CHAPTER 59

*T*he project gets finished, only costing me four or five hours of sleep. On Saturday the family comes over for Easter. Well, half of the family, the quiet half. You see, my mom's side of the family, the James side, is fairly quiet and subdued. They are a family of teachers and librarians who play bridge and chat about books and movies. My dad's side of the family is a different story. Simply put, they are loud. My cousins, most of them under seven years of age, form up like a pack of wolves and ravage whatever space they're set into. The aunties go about telling loud stories while the uncles retreat to the basement to watch golf or football on TV. Having Easter with both families is like having Easter on two different planets.

Today the quiet half comes over, and the day goes by well. I talk with my aunts about the plays that I've been in, and I talk to the uncles about fishing. There are two other kids, Rachel and Craig, both toddlers. They play quietly, always under the watchful eye of at least one adult. This little blessing is even more obvious since the gathering is being held at our house this year, and they manage to leave everything in one piece. After lunch I creep down to my room for a bit to flip through some magazines and listen to music. I can only handle a limited amount of my relatives at any given time. Then again, this crew is nothing like the loud half.

On Easter morning we go to church in Milaca, then head to Grandma's. My grandmother, the one who loaned me the Buick, lives in a little rambler only a mile or so from where she was born. My uncle still works the homestead, raising beef cattle and soybeans. His son, who everyone calls Iggy (even though he probably hates it), usually hangs with me throughout these gatherings. He's standing at the door of Grandma's as we arrive.

"Ig, what's new?" I ask, getting out of our car. Iggy is 14 or 15, tall, and could probably kick my ass due to his summers throwing hay bales. He shrugs.

"Not much," he says. He jerks his thumb back toward the house, "The gremlins are here."

"All of 'em?"

"I think so," he replies. "It's getting hard to keep track of them these days. Sometimes it's hard to tell who belongs to who." I nod. He holds out a basket of plastic eggs. "We're on Easter egg duty."

"Are we hiding them this year?"

He nods, "Yeah, but first we have to fill 'em." He picks up a plastic bag full of assorted candy.

"Where are we going?" I ask.

He shrugs, "We can't go in the house or the kids will see it. How about the garage?" I follow him inside. As he dumps the candy and eggs into two piles I find a couple of folding chairs.

"These work?"

"Thanks," he replies, sitting down. As we stuff the eggs, I take a look around the garage. All of the walls are packed with junk. Shelves upon shelves of highway cones, transmission parts, and rusty tools line every inch of wall space.

"Do you think Grandma will ever use any of this stuff?" I ask.

"Nah," Iggy says, shaking his head. "Most of it is Uncle Ben's. He keeps talking about moving it, but I don't think he every will."

"I don't get it. Why does he have all this stuff? What is its intended purpose?"

Iggy gives another shrug, "He's just a pack rat I guess." We stuff in eggs in silence for a while.

"Was the Easter Bunny good to you?" I ask.

"Yeah, he left me a Playstation game and some droppings."

"Droppings?"

He nods. "Chocolate-covered peanuts."

"Ah."

Eventually we finish with the eggs and work our way outside. We divide them into two bags and set off in opposite directions, covering as much ground as possible. With kids of different ages and abilities participating, planning an egg hunt is a complicated ordeal. First of all, you need assistance from those inside the house to keep the kids away from the windows. Without this, all is lost. Then, those planting the eggs must take into account the different ages and abilities of the egg hunters. Some must be planted in the open at ground level for the little ones. The older children should be told to leave these eggs alone, under the assumption that they contain lousy candy. Then, goals must be set higher for the older ones. Eggs are placed in rain gutters, under buckets, and within patio chairs. We've been doing the egg hunts in our family for as long as I and remember, and this batch of hunters is among the best I've seen. When everything is in place we give the signal.

"Time for the egg hunt!" I yell through the screen door. Iggy and I listen as the pitter-patter of little feet storms toward us. Baskets in hand, the little cretins storm out into the yard. The adults are close behind; some to watch the little ones and others to chronicle the event for posterity with video cameras. Our part discharged, Iggy and I are content to watch, munching on some candy that we neglected to put into the eggs. Meanwhile, the egg competition is fierce.

As the adults look on, Nancy (6) smacks Petey (5) as he tries to swipe an egg she's already spotted. Nancy is scolded for using excessive force, but since it was deserved no penalty is incurred. Later on, the rules are enforced when Nancy grabs a little kid egg from the middle of the yard, and she is fined three eggs. The penalty system was my idea when I inherited the egg hunt. Hunters are moved up to planters at around 11 years of age, then taken out of the cycle at about 18. It's a good system, and without one the whole thing could slip into anarchy.

Finally, when all is said and done, the results are calculated. All of the munchkins dump out their plastic eggs and break them open. The loot is piled, sorted, counted, and recounted. Because the youngest ones are both without the ability to count and are fairly naive, they are the easiest targets to flinch candy from. Hey, I'm doing them a favor. We don't want them to rot their teeth out at such an early age.

After the egg hunt I make my required appearance with the relatives. I explain how school has been, how the play went, and assure them that I don't have a girlfriend. This done, Iggy and I catch a ride back to his house, under the pretense of checking on the cows. Once there, we grab two sodas and play video games until I have to go home. All told, it's not a bad Easter.

CHAPTER 60

*I*t's ten o'clock on Monday morning, and I'm sitting by the phone holding two slips of paper, one with Emily's phone number, the other with Sara's number. Since we have the day off, I've decided to make some calls and test the water. I'm getting sick of all of this hanging-in-limbo crap. I want some answers. The question is, who do I call first? Sara's great and everything, but is she over Dave yet? Of course she is. Well, probably not. Ah hell, how should I know? Then there's Emily; friend, or girlfriend? Or not? Why do girls have to be so complicated? They should come with a manual or something. Without thinking, I dial Sara's number.

"Hello?"

"Hi Sara."

"No, but I can get her." Damnit! It's her sister.

"Yes, thank you," I reply. Christ, I hate it when I do that. Why do they have to sound so alike? You'd think that I could...

"Hello?"

"Hi Sara, it's Will."

"Hey Will, what's up?" Ah ha, that's a good point. I might have thought of a reason for calling before I dialed her number. Damnit again.

"Not much, just trying to think of something to do. Have a good Easter?"

"Yeah, I did, actually," she replies.

"Why, did the Easter Bunny leave you something special?" She laughs.

"No, my parents quit doing that years ago." I shove my Easter basket under the desk.

"Yeah. Mine too."

"My parents got me a dozen roses on Easter morning. It's that day I was baptized," she says.

"That was nice of them."

"Yeah, roses are my favorite flower." Hmmm.

"Huh," I say. "Hey, if you don't mind me asking, how did the whole Dave thing go over?"

"Not too bad, considering the circumstances. I'm finished with him. He tried apologizing, but I didn't fall for it. It's time for bigger and better things."

"You're not going to be an angry feminist now, are you?"

"Nope."

"And your not going lesbian on me?"

She laughs. "No, I still like guys. Just not that particular one." Hah! She likes guys! I still have a chance.

"I see. Hey, speaking of dating, I don't suppose you have anyone to set Scott up with, do you?"

"No. Why?"

"Scott needs a girlfriend and I'm trying to help him out. Maybe we'll have to look out of town."

"He needs a girlfriend?" she asks, not sounding convinced.

"It would do him good. He needs a woman in his life."

She chuckles, "I guess all guys do."

"I agree. So what about you? Are you after some hot guy from out of town?" I glance at Emily's number.

"No, not really. I'm not a big fan of long-distance relationships," she says. I set Emily's number aside.

"Yeah, me neither." I reply. "I don't think they're really worth it."

"Oh no," she says. "Not again."

"What?"

"It's my mom. She's making me clean the house."

"I guess you'd better go then. You don't want to anger mother dearest."

She sighs, "Yeah, but I'd rather sit here and talk to you. I guess I should go though. Maybe I'll talk to you later?"

"I hope so. Have fun."

"Bye." And she hangs up the phone. I lean back in my chair. Things are looking up for Mr. William Larkin. I walk around the house, half pacing, looking for something to do. It feels like I have all of this energy but nothing to do with it. I have an honest chance here. She's not against men, she's looking for someone close to home, and she wanted to talk to me. I skip around a bit. That's right; she wanted to talk to me.

I settle on taking a walk. I open up our coat closet and begin to dig through it. It takes a little while, but eventually I find what I'm looking for: a pair of big black rubber boots. I plunge my feet into them. When I stand up they come to my knees and my feet wiggle around, exploring the ample space. Perfect. I throw on an old work coat and walk outside.

It's a warm April morning, with the sun fighting back against the stubborn snow. I take full advantage of my boots, splashing in and out of puddles and mud. It's a fun walk; one without any big questions to ponder or puzzles to solve. Come to think of it, it's been a long time since I've gone puddle jumping. I guess it's one of those little things that you forget about as you age, but it strikes a certain chord once it's remembered. I suppose there are lots of things like that. Hopefully I won't forget about all of them.

CHAPTER 61

The next morning I'm eager to pick up my conversation with Sara where we left off, so I find her as soon as I can.

"Hey Sara," I say, poking my head around her locker.

"Hi," she replies, not looking up.

"How was cleaning?"

"Not so good," she says, staring into her locker.

"Why, what happened?"

"It's…It's nothing."

"No, really, what happened? Is there anything I can do?"

"I doubt it. It's my mom. We got into a fight."

"How'd it start?"

"I don't know. I was cleaning the kitchen and it wasn't good enough. Then I told her how nothing seems good enough…and…things just got worse from there." The five-minute bell rings. "Anyway, I should go."

"Ok, have a good day, huh?"

"I'll try. Thanks."

"No problem." Wow, that must have been some fight. For as long as I've known her, I don't think I've ever seen her that shook up. The Dave thing threw her, but she was never this bothered by anything. I have to do something. This sounds like a job for (cue fanfare music) Perspective Boyfriend Man! All right, so I'm going to do something, but what? Candy? A card? Right. I don't think Hallmark has a "Sorry you and your mom had a fight" series. Flowers? Ah ha, flowers. Roses, more specifically. Should I order them now or later? The tardy bell rings. Now it is.

I work my way up to the pay phone and look up Milaca Floral. Since her favorite flower is the rose, it's the obvious choice, but how many? A simple rose would be classy, but there's always that special something about a dozen roses. We'll do both. I'll send her two roses an hour for the rest of the day for a grand total of a dozen. Classy.

The roses end up setting me back about fifty bucks, but it's worth it. She gets her first two roses in chemistry. Her face lights up with surprise, then wonder. I decided not to add a card, at least not at first. Eventually she'll find out it's me, and right now she might even think they're from her mom. Either way, they seem to brighten up her day.

By the time lunch rolls around the rumors have started. It's hard to receive flowers around here without causing a stir. It sounds like most people think they're from a secret admirer (which isn't entirely false), and others think they might be from her parents. I'll tell her the whole story at the end of the day, once she has the full dozen.

The afternoon passes slowly, and I have one eye on the clock the whole time. When I'm finally freed I go to my locker first, not wanting to seem too eager. Once I have my jacket and backpack I set off to find Sara. I catch up with her at her locker. She's talking to Dave. I don't want to jump into the middle of anything, so I stop a few yards away and dig through my bag, acting like I'm looking for something. From here, I can just make out what they're saying.

"I just wanted to let you know that I'm sorry," Dave says.

"Thank you," she replies. "Roses have always been my favorite flower. Weren't they expensive?" Expensive? What the hell? Wait a minute…

"So you'll think about it then?"

She nods, "Yeah, I just need a little time."

"All right," he replies. He leans in to kiss her, but she turns away. Good sign. His business apparently finished, he walks away. I can't believe he's trying to cash in on my idea, and on top of that he's trying to get back with Sara! It's somewhat insulting actually. It's time to set the record straight.

"What did Dave want?" I ask, walking over to Sara.

She shrugs, "He just wanted to apologize for being a jerk." I'd think it would have taken longer than that. "He wants to get back together with me."

"And?"

She shakes her head, "It's not going to happen." I start breathing again. "We're just not right for each other."

"What's the story with all of the flowers?" I ask, pointing to the bundle in her locker.

"Dave said they're from him, but I don't believe it." My heart skips a beat. "They're probably from my mom." Blast. Another moral quandary. I suppose it would be nice if I let her think they're from her mom, but she'll probably find out eventually. I might as well break the news to her.

"It wasn't your mom either," I say, giving her a little smile.

"What do you mean?"

"Well, you sounded upset about the whole thing with your mom, and I knew roses were your favorite flower, so I thought they might brighten up your day."

"You did this?" I nod. "Oh Will," she says, giving me a big hug. "You didn't have to do that! Thank you."

"No problem. I have a question for you though. Why do you believe me and not Dave?"

She pauses for a second, then smiles. "Because you, Sir William, are not an arrogant ass."

"Thank you, Lady Fuller."

"Would you care to escort me to my car, kind sir?"

"I would be delighted." I walk her to her car, wondering if I have the guts to ask her out. It shouldn't be a big deal, just be casual. Is she busy this Friday? Ask her, it couldn't hurt. Come on, the flowers put me into golden territory, and an opportunity like this doesn't come along very often. Ask.

We get to her car. She opens the door and tosses her bag inside, then carefully sets the flowers on the passenger seat. Should I? Yes. Well, maybe not. How should I know? Why is she looking at me like that?

"Is there something you wanted to tell me?" she asks, cocking her head.

"No," I say. "Well, maybe. Why do you ask?"

"It looks like you have something on your mind, that's all." Damn, she's got me. Ok, go.

"Actually, I do. I was wondering if you're doing anything this Friday."

"I don't think so, why?"

"I wanted to know if you want to go see a movie or something."

She puts her hands on her hips. "Will, are you asking me out on a date?"

I blush. "Maybe."

"Well it's about time," she replies. Then she gets into her car and slams the door shut.

"Wait!" I say, plastering my face up against the window. "Is that a yes or a no?"

"Yes," she says through the glass. "But on one condition."

"What?"

"I choose the movie." Then she pulls away, almost running over my foot in the process. I suppose it doesn't matter, I'm too stunned to reply, even if I would be given the chance.

CHAPTER 62

❀

*W*hen I see Sara the next day I'm not quite sure how to act. Sure, we're seeing a movie this weekend, but does that mean she's my girlfriend? There should be a book about this sort of thing. "The Guy's Guide to High School Relationships." The authors would make millions.

She finds me before chemistry. Out of the corner of my eye I see her sit down. She looks beautiful. That's my girlfriend over there...I think. She looks at me, waiting for me to come over and talk to her. I'm forced ignore her for a little while, furiously finishing up the lab report that's due today.

"Sorry," I say, finally finishing. "I figured I should get this done before the bell rings."

She nods, "I finished it up last night." I pause for a second, wondering if I should ask the question. Why not? My luck has been pretty good lately.

"Sara," I say, looking around for eavesdroppers, "Can I ask you a question?"

"Of course."

"Well, since we're seeing a movie together this weekend, that would be considered a date, right?"

She smiles. "I hope so."

"So we're dating. Does that mean you're my girlfriend?"

She shifts in her chair a bit. "Well, I'd say that we're dating, but I wouldn't call you my boyfriend."

I wish this stuff wasn't so confusing. "So when does that line get crossed?" Man, I sound like an idiot. Do most people know these things?

She giggles. "I'll be sure to let you know." SEE!? Girls seem to know all about this, why don't guys? It must have something to do with that other X chromosome or something. I decide to bring up the matter at lunch.

"I heard you asked Sara out," Adam says as he sits down at the lunch table. I'm actually surprised it took so long for the news to reach him.

"Well, sort of," I reply.

"What do you mean?"

"Hold on. Scott, Richard, come here," I say. I only want to tell the story once. They sit down and I start to explain. "Here's the deal. I asked Sara to a movie on Friday, and she accepted." A few approving nods are passed around the table. "But there's a problem. I asked her today, and she said that we're dating, but she's not my girlfriend."

"Wait a minute," Scott interrupts, "You asked her?"

"Yeah. Hell, I didn't know. Anyway, how do I tell the difference?" The question is met only with shrugs. I sigh, "That's what I thought too."

Aaron speaks up, "Does this have anything to do with the roses?"

I grin. "Yep, that was me."

Richard looks puzzled. "Roses? What roses?"

I turn to him. "I sent Sara a dozen roses yesterday. It was all over the school, didn't you hear about it?"

"No, I didn't know. I need to find a loop."

"A what?"

Richard sighs. "It seems like everyone has a loop that keeps them up to date on stuff like that, but I'm outside of all the loops."

I shrug, "So get yourself a loop." The conversation carries on from there, touching on issues like girls' necklines, the feasibility of robots in the home, and the ability of the school's rolls to soak up chocolate milk. For the record, the little buggers can soak up almost half a carton.

CHAPTER 63

❋

The next two days go by quickly, and before I know it it's Friday night. After much deliberation about what to wear, I settle on a ribbed sweater; not too dressy, not too casual, and nice and soft for any cuddling that may occur. I drive over to pick her up. She lives on a little hobby farm on the other side of town, and as I pull up her driveway I almost hit her dog. That's not exactly the way I'd like to start our newfound relationship. Once my breathing returns to normal, I park the Buick and get out. My palms sweat as I work my way up the muddy sidewalk, wondering what her parents will be like. I've met them before, but I wasn't dating their daughter at the time.

"Oh, hi Will," her mom says as she opens the door. "Sara is just finishing up upstairs, she should be down in just a minute." She gestures for me to come in, so I step inside. I dread what may happen next. What if I have to talk to her mom for half an hour? What if she quizzes me on all the biggies; grades, friends, religion, careers, and the future? I'm bound to slip up somewhere.

"Hi Will," Sara says as she comes down the stairs. My blood pressure drops 50 points. "Sorry to keep you waiting."

"No problem," I reply. Liar.

"Well, you two have fun," her mom says, walking off toward the kitchen.

"We will," we reply.

When we get to the movie theatre, I realize that I have no idea as to what we've spent the last half hour talking about. We must have talked about something, because I don't recall any noticeable silent spells, but I couldn't tell you what we talked about. This causes a bit of a concern, if only for the fact that if she told me something important I don't think I'll remember it.

The fair maiden has selected a chic flick for our night on the town, Ten Things I Hate About You. I don't even argue. I know what you're thinking, and I'm not whipped, I just choose my battles wisely. This is not my battle.

"I think Dots are the perfect movie candy," she says as we get to our seats. I scoff at her. "What?" she says.

"Dots? They're just little balls of gelatin. Now Junior Mints, there's a perfect movie snack.

"Or they would be," she adds, "If they didn't have the mint stuff in them."

"Nonsense."

"Really," she says, "I mean come on, the stuff looks horrible."

"Who's arguing aesthetics? I don't care what the inside looks like, they taste great."

She shrugs, "They're all right." Dots, honestly. Then it dawns on me; we just had our first argument. She had an opinion. I had an opinion. They weren't the same, and that was ok! "What are you smiling about?" she asks.

"Nothing," I reply, moving a little closer to her. "It's nothing."

Soon thereafter the theatre gets dark and the previews begin. I'm faced with an important first date question: should I or should I not put my arm around her? I have the sweater working to my advantage, and it does bring about that whole closeness feeling, but it may seem a bit too forward. I could always go with hand holding instead. We'll play it safe. I inch my arm onto the armrest. She has both of her hands folded in her lap, yielding a significant logistics problem. I need to get her to put her arm next to mine, but putting my hand in her lap can't be the best option. I'm guessing that it would be frowned upon. I slide my elbow to the very edge of the armrest, hoping to make it look more inviting. Success! She slides her arm up next to mine. Now for the tricky part.

I pull my hand away and pop a Junior Mint into my mouth, then set my hand back on the armrest, this time directly on top of hers. She gives me a little squeeze with her thumb. I should patent that move. Later on, I decide to go for the arm-around-the-shoulders bit. I consider the "yawn and stretch" maneuver, but opt for the direct route instead. When I put my arm around her shoulder she snuggles closer, like she was expecting it. Nice.

About an hour into the movie I run into another snag. Though I like cuddling and having her close to me, I'm starting to loose circulation in my arm. It's really starting to hurt. Wonderful. I have to figure out some way to free my arm, but still keep her close to me. Watching a movie really shouldn't be this difficult. I could offer her some Junior Mints, but she doesn't really like them. She's holding the Dots so that wouldn't work either. Forget about it, that's all I can do. It's not so bad, all I have to do is ignore it. No problem at all.

I can't ignore it. A guy can only withstand pins and needles for so long.

"If you don't mind," I say, taking back my appendage, "My arm is starting to fall asleep."

"Oh, sorry," she says.

"Don't worry about it." And we're back to hand holding. I like this date.

After the movie we swing by Java Z for coffee. I have my cup of the house blend, she orders some latte mocha cappuccino conglomeration.

"How can you drink that stuff?" she asks as we sit down.

"Like this," I reply, taking another sip.

"But it's so bitter."

I shake my head. "It's real coffee."

"As opposed to what?"

"As opposed to that fu-fu stuff you're drinking."

"Hey," she says, pointing a finger at me, "Lay off the turtle mocha." We'll call this one a draw. We find an open couch and sit down to talk. We chat for quite some time, becoming quite comfortable with each other (although not quite as comfortable as Julie tended to get). Since we don't want to break curfew, we are forced to leave much too soon.

When we get back to her house I realize that I have no idea as to what I should do next. For one thing, we have to sign up for the prom sometime soon. If we want to get in I've got to ask her in the near future. Then there is the matter of a goodnight kiss. Do I take charge of the matter? Would that be too pushy?

"So, are you going to prom?" I ask as we pull up the driveway.

"I was hoping to," she replies.

"Hoping to?"

"Nobody's asked me yet." An invitation if I've ever heard one. Then again, I don't want to be shot down. A little more beating about the bush will be necessary.

"Can I ask you a hypothetical question?" I say, turning off the Buick.

"Of course."

"If a guy such as myself asked a girl such as yourself to prom, do you think she'd go with him?"

She smiles, "I think so."

"Fair enough. Can I ask you another question?"

"Sure."

"Will you go to prom with me?"

"Yes, I'd love to." Do I kiss her or not, do I kiss her or not? She gets out of the car. I guess not. I walk her to her door, holding her hand. "I had a good time tonight," she says.

"Me too." The crucial moment. She turns her head up just a little bit, then looks from my eyes to my lips. This is it.

I notice something moving out of the corner of my eye. I tear my eyes away from her gaze for just an instant and I see them. Both of Sara's sisters are in the living room, peaking over the bottom of the windows. Cretins. Sara's brow furrows.

"I guess this is goodnight," she says.

"Sweet dreams," I say, and she walks inside. Stupid sisters. When I get back to my car I realize that I didn't ask my other question. Is she my girlfriend yet? I suppose time will tell.

CHAPTER 64

So, I've finally got myself a prom date. It's a bit depressing to think that getting a date is only the first step.

"Allison!" I yell, catching up with her in the commons after school. "Help me."

"With what?"

"Prom."

"You're going?"

"With Sara, what about you?" She replies with a guilty grin. "Really? With who?"

"His name is Nate. I met him in St. Cloud."

"You guys dating?" I ask. "Are you sure about this one Al?"

She shakes her head, "We're just going as friends. Anyway, what do you need help with?"

"Everything. I have a date. Now what?"

She just sighs and leads me over to a table. "Sit down." I do. "We have a lot of work to do. I'm sure she's all worked up about her end of the deal, but don't worry about her. First of all, you're going to need a tuxedo. Then you need to set up transportation."

"I have a car."

She rolls her eyes, "You are not picking her up in the battleship. You'll also need dinner reservations. Then what are you planning to do after dinner?" I shrug. She sighs, "I'm glad you came to me as soon as you did. Let's see, how about this; our neighbors were planning on letting us use their hot tub, but it sounds like we're going down to St. Paul instead. Would you want to use it?" Would I ever.

"Yeah, that'd be great."

"Then that's settled. You'll want to rent a tux somewhere in St. Cloud, but what about the car?"

I think for a second. "I have an uncle who has a Mercedes."

"Does he like you?"

"He has to, he's my godfather."

She laughs, "Ok, done. What about dinner?"

"The Olive Garden?"

She shakes her head, "Too cliché."

"What about a picnic by the hot tub?"

"Much better."

I sigh. "Wow. We just figured out prom."

"Not so fast," she replies. "You're not done yet."

"What do you mean?"

She drops a pile of magazines on the table, "I still have to find a dress." I shrug and sit back down. I didn't even know there was a Prom Magazine. What is this world coming to? "Just mark the ones you like," she says.

"You got it." Honestly, it's not too bad of a job. There are lots of worse things to be doing than looking at hot girls in prom dresses. Once all of the magazines are combed through we compare notes. Any dress that either one of us objects to is thrown out, and after considerable discussion only a handful remain.

"There. That wasn't so bad," she says.

"Yeah, I don't really mind picking out dresses."

Allison gives me a sideways glance, "Don't get too attached to it. I don't want to see you trying on prom dresses at Macy's or anything."

I nod, "I'll try and resist the temptation."

CHAPTER 65

*T*hursday afternoon finds Sara and I in the parking lot by her car. It's a bit of a chivalry that I've taken to, walking her to her car every day. I should have been a knight.

"Will, I need to tell you something," she says.

"What is it?"

"I can't make it this Friday." Yes, that's right, we had another date planned.

"Why not?"

"Mom's taking me shopping in the cities. We're going down there for the weekend." Daaaamn. I was actually going to cook dinner and everything. Tomorrow is when she's supposed to meet my parents.

"Oh." I reply. "That's too bad."

"I'll give you a rain check, ok?"

"Sure." Damn scheduling.

"What's wrong?"

"Nothing."

"No really, what is it?" Wow, she really looks concerned. This is kind of nice.

"It's just that I was planning on having you meet my parents tomorrow. I was going to make dinner."

"Aww, she says, "I'm sorry. Can we do it next week?" I nod. "Thanks for understanding." Then she leans in and kisses me. It takes me by surprise, but it's a welcome one. I kiss her back, holding it as long as I can before we break away. Wow. Sara opens her car door. "And for future reference," she says, "I would love to be your girlfriend."

I smile, "Then I suppose I wouldn't object to being called your boyfriend."

"I'll talk to you tomorrow," she says, hops into her car, and pulls away; leaving me standing in her parking space, hovering slightly above the ground.

On Friday I inform Scott of the whole ordeal.

"Sounds like things went pretty well," he says.

"Yeah, I suppose."

"You suppose? You got a kiss from the girl you've had a crush on for almost a year, the girl you've been running odds on, that girl; and you suppose?"

I guess he has a point. "But there's a thing," I protest.

"A thing?"

"Well, I guess it was the whole Julie fiasco. I'm a little gun shy. Maybe it's too soon."

Scott shakes his head, "No. Don't do this to yourself. You don't get to mess things up this time."

"This time? What are you talking about?"

"Nothing. Just listen to me: do not let her go."

"Yeah," I say, "You're right."

"Of course I am. Now let's get lunch." And it's settled. As I eat I reflect on the whole situation. I can't argue, the kiss was good, and it's something I've been hoping for. And this really is a good relationship. The fact that I had doubts worries me though. Maybe they'll always be there, those little voices in the back of my head. Then again, if the whole kissing thing keeps up, it might be just the thing to shut those voices up.

CHAPTER 66

*I*n my mind weekends are for resting and for sleeping in. For the most part it works out that way, but not this weekend. This weekend Dad and I are opening up the cabin for the year. Now that the ice is off the lake and the leaves are on the trees it's time to get the cabin ready for the summer. The biggest chore of the weekend is putting in docks. Every year I dread it, because the docks never go in smoothly. Things wouldn't be so bad if we only had one dock to put in, but here we have two docks, two lifts, and a handful of walkways from shore to the main docks.

The cabin is first. When we get to the lake Dad and I go about opening it up. We pull open shades, turn on the heat, and open up a few windows to let some air in. Our cabin is a fairly small building with only one bedroom. My bed is on the screened three-season porch that faces the lake, which suits me just fine. I'd rather sleep on the screened in porch, listening to the waves, than in any bedroom.

Once the cabin is finished Dad and I turn to the docks. For most people putting in docks isn't a big deal, they just roll them into the water. For us, it presents a bit more of a problem. Our cabin sits on a fifty-foot hill overlooking Mille Lacs Lake, preventing us from just letting anything roll in. Instead, we must tie them to our truck with a huge rope and slowly lower them down to the water.

Before we do all this we must first gather up our equipment. One high-lift jack, one heavy rope, two socket wrenches, and two long metal bars are all laid out along the shoreline. Dad and I climb into our neoprene chest waders, call the neighbor, Bud, over to drive the truck, and the ordeal begins.

Overall, the whole thing doesn't go too badly. There is a considerable amount of yelling when I almost drop a dock section on Dad's foot, and I have to dig around in forty-degree water when I drop a wrench, but things could be worse. Then a wave crests over the top of my waders.

"Ohmygodthatscold!" I yell as ice water pours into my waders.

"What happened?" Dad asks as he bolts two sections together. I reply with a few assorted gasps. "What happened?"

"Waders…filled…with…water," I squeeze out. "I've gotta get out of these," I say, staggering to shore.

"You'll be fine. We just have to place one more dock and we'll be done," he snaps. I can actually feel my legs freezing.

"No, I'm pulling these off." I'm so cold it hurts.

"Fine!" he yells, hurling his wrench to shore, "Then you can finish it yourself!" I ignore him, hustling up the steps to the cabin. After a long, hot shower I return to the water, only to find the docks fully assembled.

"Thanks," I say to Dad as he walks by, carrying the jack and wrenches back to the tool shed.

"Don't mention it," he mutters. Sensing that I'm already on thin ice, I don't ask him to help me with my sailboat.

My boat is a sixteen foot Windrider Trimiran, a three-hulled craft that is capable of taking the beating that this lake can dish out. It's made out of a high-density plastic, the same stuff that makes up whitewater kayaks, and she's supposed to be unsinkable. I haven't proven them wrong yet. She can carry three people, one sailing the boat from the cockpit in the center hull and two sitting on either side of him on the nets that are strung between the hulls. The single sail wraps around the mast for storage, and we keep the whole contraption on a modified boatlift off of one of our docks.

Assembling the boat isn't particularly difficult, but it takes awhile. By the time I'm done with the hulls, the mast, and the rigging, an hour has past. There is a slight breeze coming from the south, so I decide to take her out for a spin. The water is still freezing, but with enough polar-fleece and rain gear I should be able to stay dry.

I work my way back up to the cabin and strap on my armor, er, my rain gear. Once I'm strapped into the cockpit of my craft I push off. As I get clear of land and the docks I catch the breeze, letting it fill my sail and whisk me across the surface of the waves.

It seems like forever since I've been out on the water. I've always liked to sail, it offers me my own little sanctuary. Out here, no one can get to me. My boat ghosts across the surface of the water, the only sound coming from the wake I leave behind. When I get past Hawkbill Point the full force of the wind hits me. The force drives the downwind hull underwater and shoots the boat across the lake. This boat, with its narrow bow and sharp edges, tends to cut through waves instead of going over them. At times it's nice, preventing the boat from rocking too much in a chop. Other times, it's not so nice. Today every other wave seems to douse me with a spray of icy water. The rain jacket keeps me dry for a while, but soon enough I feel the water creeping its way down my neck and chest. It doesn't matter much though. For the most part there has to be ice on the water to keep me off this lake.

CHAPTER 67

The next Monday Sara approaches me at lunch, catching me by surprise.

"Hey Will," she says, poking her head between Scott and I. "Do you have a minute?"

I look around, "Sara, what are you doing here? Shouldn't you be in class?"

She shrugs, "I told them I had to go to the bathroom. Can I talk to you?"

"Sure," I say, standing up. I point at an empty table, "Over there?" She nods. It must be serious, we always talk in front of the guys. She's smiling though. Odd.

"I couldn't wait to tell you," she says, sitting down. "A few months ago I sent in an audition tape for a select choir that's going to be traveling around Europe this summer, and I was accepted!"

"Hey, that's great!" I say, giving her a hug. "When did you find out?"

"Mr. Johnson just told me in class. I've got to get working on the music though, we leave on May 20th."

"Where do you get to go?"

"We go through England, Spain, France, Germany, and Italy," she says, ticking each one off on her fingers.

"Wow, how long are you going to be gone?"

"Four weeks."

"Whoa. Come again?"

"We're gone for four weeks."

"So you won't get back until July?"

"That's right." She glances at the wall clock, "But listen, I've got to get back to class. I'll talk to you later?"

"Yeah," I reply. I walk back to my lunch table. "Damn."

"What was that about?" Scott asks, poking his chicken on rice around his plate.

"It's Sara. She was accepted into some choir that's traveling Europe this summer."

"Well, that's good," he replies.

"It's not that great. It means that she'll be gone for four weeks, the end of May and all of June."

"Long time," Aaron chimes in.

"No kidding," I reply, "And who knows what's going to happen. She'll be traveling with a bunch of high school kids for a month, I'm sure there's bound to be some guys going along."

"I see what you mean," Scott says, "You're not sure if she'll remember her boy back home." I shrug. "So now what?"

I smile, "I guess I'll just have to give her something to remember before she goes."

Scott arches an eyebrow, "Such as?"

"Well, prom is coming up," I say, considering my options. "That has some potential. Then we have our one-month anniversary the day before she leaves. I guess I'll just have to make it an event she'll remember."

"Have anything planned?"

I grin, "I'm sure I'll think of something."

CHAPTER 68

"This is so pointless," I mutter as I flip through my social textbook. "Honestly, how does this prepare us for the real world?"

Allison looks up from her book, "It teaches us to be able to perform worthless, menial jobs. Welcome to the world of middle management."

"I promise you, when I get a job it won't be slogging through textbooks to find answers to a worksheet; that's for sure." I say, tapping my pencil on the desk.

"Ok," Al says, "What would be better for preparing us for the real world?"

"Life 101," I reply, "A class about life."

"What do you mean?"

"Well, one day you could have a class about general car care. The next day you could talk about how to balance a checkbook or how to barbeque ribs. And there would have to be a week or two dedicated to understanding the opposite sex."

"I'd take the class," she says, "But I think I'm starting to understand the whole opposite sex thing on my own."

"Oh?"

She smiles, "Yeah, I met a guy."

I shake my head, "This can't be good."

"No, it's great," she says. "His name is Charles, and he is a true gentlemen. He went to military school before his parents split up, and he does everything in perfect form. I mean, he's not the kind of guy who would eat peanut butter and jelly sandwiches, but if he did, he'd use a different knife for both the peanut butter and the jelly." She sighs. "He treats me like a lady, he even opens his car doors for me."

"Maybe he has a new car. How long have you known this guy?"

"A week or so, but it feels like so much longer."

"What about prom?"

"Nate said it'd be fine if I went with someone else, and Charles said he'd be honored to take me."

I sigh, "Well, I'm happy for you Al."

"Thanks."

"But be careful, ok?"

"Aww," she says, "Thanks big brother."

"Shut up," I reply, trying to hide a smile. "I'm just trying to keep an eye on you."

"Will," she says, not smiling this time. "Really. Thanks."

I nod. "Don't mention it."

The rest of the day trudges along, dragging me with it. The realization that I'm halfway through the week doesn't help much, especially when it's paired with tomato soup and a grilled cheese sandwich for lunch. I hate tomato soup.

"You all ready for prom?" Scott asks as I sit down at the lunch table. I drop my head.

"Damnit. Ugh, of course I'm not ready. I was supposed to pick up my tuxedo last night. It's still at the rental place."

Scott shakes his head, "You'd better get on it. What about you, Richard?"

"I'm not going," he says, picking the crust off his sandwich.

"Why not? I thought we were all going. Well, except for Aaron," Scott says, pointing toward the freshman.

"Wait," I say, holding up my hand. "Paul, you're going?" He nods. "With who, your not girlfriend?"

He shrugs, "Yeah, I asked Amy."

"And the good reverend is letting you take his daughter to a dance? I'm shocked."

"It's not all that great," he replies, "I still have to get her home by midnight."

"Or she'll turn back into a peasant?" Aaron asks.

"Nope," Paul says, crumpling up his lunch bag. "But I doubt we can roll that giant pumpkin all the way home from St. Cloud."

CHAPTER 69

On Thursday Sara comes over to study for our biology test tomorrow. When I made the request to my parents I got about the answer I expected. She can come over, but we can't study in my room at all. I can understand their concern, but I really don't think we'll be rolling around on the floor making out. Not quite yet, at least.

Dad is there when we get home. Sara just decided to follow me in her car to make things easier when she leaves. Being the proper gentleman that I am, I make sure to take her coat when we get inside the house.

"Hi guys," Dad says as he pokes his head out of the kitchen. "Do you want anything to eat?" It's strange how nice my dad can be when other people are around.

"No, I'm fine Mr. Larkin," Sara replies. We lug our backpacks into the living room and drop onto the couch.

"Do you want to get right to work?" I ask.

She responds with a sly grin. "Maybe not right away."

"Well, my dad is still in the kitchen," I say, looking around.

"Not that!" she says, hitting my arm. She pulls out a handful of magazines. "This."

"What is it?" I ask, sliding closer to her.

"Prom dresses," she says, flipping through one of the magazines.

"Oh. You don't have your prom dress?" I ask. Great, my prom date will be wearing a dishrag. Wait a minute…

"I have my dress, silly. I just figured that as long as I'm looking through them I might want to pick one out for prom next year."

I smile, Cheshire-like. "Well, that would help me pick out my cummerbund I guess."

She lifts an eyebrow, "Maybe you won't be the one dancing with me." Ouch. "What do you think of this one?" she asks, pointing to a blue strapless dress with a huge skirt.

"A bit bridesmaid-ish," I reply. After going through this with Al I have a pretty good idea of what I'm looking for.

"And this?" A lacy, form fitting lavender number.

"Nice," I say. She folds the corner of the page over.

"What about this one?" she asks, pointing out an orange two-piece.

"Ugh," is my reply. "I don't think any girl should be allowed to wear a two-piece, they should stay on the beach. That one looks like an orange cut in half."

Her eyes narrow. "This is my dress for this year," she snaps. Shit. I try to think of something to say, but nothing comes. "I'm sorry if I look like a sliced orange," she says, picking up her backpack.

"No Sara, I was…I was kidding," I plead, trying to save myself. It doesn't help.

"Save it," she says, pulling on her coat. "I don't want to hear any of it." With that she turns on her heels and walks out the door. Dad walks out of the kitchen.

"Where'd Sara go?" he asks.

"Uh, she remembered that she had to get home for supper," I say.

He smiles. "I hope she doesn't eat too much. Those two-piece dresses are pretty to squeeze into." I just ignore him and turn back to my biology.

CHAPTER 70

Operation Save Will's Ass is now fully in effect. Prom is in just a few days, and I can't let Sara be mad at me now. I have to salvage things as soon as I can.

I park my car at the end of Sara's driveway and quietly close the door. I don't want to be making a lot of noise at 9:30 at night; her dad probably shoots prowlers. As I work my way up the driveway I start to have second thoughts. This kind of thing always seems to work in movies, but I've begun to realize that what happens in movies usually has no bearing whatsoever on what happens in my life.

When I reach the house I see that it's mostly dark; the only lights are in the master bedroom and in Sara's room. Perfect. I pick a few pebbles from the driveway and walk under Sara's window. Here we go. I fling the first pebble up at her window, hoping to get her attention. Instead, it ricochets off the siding with a dull **thunk.** The wind took it, I swear. I try the next pebble, a smaller one this time. **Pa-think.** Success! I take a deep breath, expecting to see Sara come to the window at any second. Nothing happens.

Ok, so I'll use a bigger rock. I pick out a stone the size of a marble and hurl it at her window. **Plink**! She must have heard that one. My heart skips a beat as I see her shadow approach the window. The shades lift and I see her standing there in jeans and a hooded sweatshirt. She looks beautiful. She opens the window and looks outside.

"Is someone there?" she says, her voice shaking slightly.

"It's me," I say in a loud whisper, waving my arms.

"What are you doing here?" she says, not altogether pleased with me.

"But soft! What light through yonder window breaks? It is the East, and Juliet is the sun!"

"What are you doing?"

I bend down on one knee. "She speaks! O, speak again, bright angel, for thou art as glorious to this night, being o'er my head, as a winged messenger of heaven."

She shakes her head. "You are such a dork."

"Shall I hear more, or shall I speak at this?"

She laughs, "Keep talking, Romeo."

"With love's light wings did I o'erpearch these walls; for stony limits cannot hold love out, and what love can do, that dares love attempt. Therefore thy kinsmen are no stop to me."

"Do you know what my dad would do if he saw you here?" she whispers. I love it when things come together like this.

"I have night's cloak to hide me from their eyes. And but thou love me, let them find me here. My life were better ended by their hate than death prorogued, wanting of thy love."

"And what's that supposed to mean?" she asks, starting to sound playful.

"It means don't be mad at me. I like oranges."

"Oh do you?"

"Yes, m'lady, they are my favorite fruit."

She laughs. I am a genius. Then the lights begin to turn on.

"Sara, are you talking to someone?" her dad calls.

"Go!" she whispers at me. "No Dad!" she yells back to him. "I'm just practicing my presentation for school tomorrow." Nice save. As I run back down the driveway I consider going back for a goodnight kiss, but then realize that it'd be suicidal. I'd be gored by a rosebush before I'd ever make it to the window.

CHAPTER 71

"Did you get things all set up for tomorrow?" Scott asks, pulling his books out of his locker.

"Yeah, Allison's neighbors are still letting us use their hot tub, and my uncle is dropping off his car at our house this afternoon."

"Do your parents know about the hot tub?"

"Well, sorta." He gives me a sideways glance. "I told them Allison is having a little shindig at her house and that we're invited. That much is true; we just happen to be the only two there."

"An omission of truth may still be considered a lie," says a voice from behind me. I turn around to see Bish leaning up against another locker. "I'm sure your parental unit would not approve."

I shrug, "What they don't know won't hurt them."

"That's not completely true, but it's your decision. Mr. Lane, what are your plans for the evening?"

"There's a big after-prom thing going on a the golf course, I think we're going there. What about you?"

"I helped coordinate the event," Bish replies, "I am content with overseeing the evolution of my creation."

"Wait," I say, "You don't have a date?"

"Correct." Wow. Of all people, Bish is the last one I'd expect not to have a date. "By choice," he adds, "Not be default. I did not want anything to distract me. That and I do not want anyone to get jealous." That grin makes me want to press the issue, but knowing Bish he'll leave it at that. Then I get an idea.

"Mr. Bishop, can I ask you a favor?"

"Certainly."

"You see, I'd like to make tomorrow night special for Sara, especially after the whole dress fiasco."

"And?"

"And I need a driver. I'm borrowing my uncle's Mercedes for the evening, and a personal driver would complete the package."

"Mr. Larkin, say no more. I would be honored, but on one condition."

"Anything."

"You will repay me with a favor when the time comes."

Scenes from The Godfather flash through my mind, but I nod in agreement. "Done. Oh, one more thing. Could you dress nice for the whole thing? I want to make a good impression."

Bish pauses for a moment, and then smiles, "I have a tuxedo perfect for the occasion. Good day gentlemen." That settled, Bish continues down the hall.

"So what do you think will come from this hot tub setup?" Scott asks.

"What do you mean?"

"Prom night. Girlfriend. Hot tub. You can't say nothing is going to happen."

"What?" I say, "You think we're going to have sex or something?"

He shrugs, "I doubt you haven't thought about it. I'll bet she has."

"No way. She's not like that."

He flips his locker shut. "All right, if you say so." Honestly, I hadn't even thought about sex as a possibility, much less about what I would do if put in a situation like that. I don't think I could handle any more complications in my life; I have enough trouble with the one's I've got. Sometimes things would be so much easier if Scott would just shut up about stuff like this. Now the plague of the what-ifs is upon me again.

CHAPTER 72

It is five minutes before the beginning of Grand March and I'm putting on my shoes, getting ready to walk out of the house. This is bad. It's not my fault, really, it's not. At some point last night Mom must have decided that my shirt needs to be ironed. On it's own that wouldn't be a very big deal, but she didn't put it back in my closet. As a result, I spent twenty minutes tearing apart the house to find the damn thing.

My car hits 90 on the way to school; at least I think it does. The speedometer only goes to 85, and I'm accelerating when I hit that. Of course when I get to the school the parking lot is full, so I have to park on a side street two blocks away. It's hard to run in a tuxedo.

"Where have you been!?" Sara hisses as I rush in the door.

"Long story, let's go," I say, pulling her toward the gym. We find the line of students near the door and take our places. When we're finally situated I take my first good look at Sara. She looks like a princess. I lean over and whisper to her "You look beautiful." She looks me up and down.

"You're not so bad yourself," she replies. It's strange, looking around, to see all of these people who I go to class with now wearing tuxes and dresses. I wave to Allison and prince charming. Al looks good when she's all cleaned up. I don't know if I've ever seen her dressed up before. The boyfriend, on the other hand, looks like he was born in a tuxedo.

Julie is here too, with yet another new guy. She seems to be changing boyfriends as fast as I change socks. Dave is here too, being his usual parasitic self. You would think he could refrain from groping his date for just an hour or so; it shouldn't be too much to ask.

Eventually it's our turn to walk across the gym. It's an exhilarating feeling, escorting Sara across the floor. It feels good, really good, to know that after all of these screwed up relationships I finally have something that is going well.

The whole program is over in a blur. Sara and I say our goodbyes; she's on her way to Ann's house to do their hair and makeup and all other manners of things. It's strange; I have no desire whatsoever to get together with my friends and do my hair and put on cologne. Try as I might, I don't think I'll ever understand girls.

"Hey Scott," I say, catching him on the way to his car, "What are you doing before the dance tonight?"

He shrugs, "Just heading home I guess. The girls are getting ready and everything, but I don't really have anything planned. You?"

"Not sure. Bish is coming over later, you could come hang out with us if you want."

"I might. I'll see you tonight," he replies. I wave him off and walk to my own car, fiddling with my cufflinks. The fact that I'm already nervous is a little unsettling.

CHAPTER 73

$\mathcal{I}$ feel surprisingly calm as the big black Mercedes slides up Sara's driveway. I'm quickly growing fond of the inky chariot, I just might have to pick one up sometime. Bish has gone all out tonight. He's wearing a full tux with a top hat and spats; the best dressed butler that I've ever seen. When we pull up to her house Bish stops the car and gets out.

"Your lady awaits," he says, opening my door. As he waits by the car I walk up to the house. Sara's mom is there waiting for me.

"Oh don't you look so handsome? Come on inside and we'll have to get some pictures of the two of you," she says, pulling me through the door. Sara is there too, standing in the entryway. However many hours spent over at Ann's paid off; she looks radiant. With her hair all pinned, clipped, and curled, it looks like my girlfriend just stepped out of Vogue Magazine. Cool.

We pose for a few pictures for Ms. Fuller, but Sara's dad is nowhere to be found. I guess it's for the better. I can't imagine what it must be like for a father to have his daughter taken out to prom. The worst-case scenarios are endless.

"Is that Bishop?" Sara asks as we walk toward the car.

"Nope," I reply. "That's my driver, Jeeves."

"Yeah right. Hi Bish." He doesn't reply, he merely opens the car door for her.

"Thank you, Jeeves," I tell him.

"Certainly sir," comes the reply. I'll have to remember to tip him handsomely.

We don't talk much on the way to prom. There are little snippets of conversation concerning the dance, who will be there, who won't, and what we're doing afterwards. I decided to keep our after-prom activities secret until we're done with the dance. It adds an element of suspense, but it was hard to get her swimsuit without her knowing. I managed though; it's in the trunk with the rest of our stuff. I was honestly considering "not packing" her swimsuit to see what she'd do. My better judgment argued against it though, figuring that she might just go home. That's not something I want to risk.

We arrive at the dance fashionably late, about half an hour after the start. Some people are still arriving, but the gala event is already in full swing. Jeeves escorts us to the front doors, where we step out of a warm spring evening and into...an ocean? Impressive. The prom committee has gone with an "under the sea" theme for this year, and they've done quite well for themselves.

The decorations are tasteful and well thought out, unlike some disasters of past years. The decorating committee has finally realized that even though we have a theme, it doesn't have to be overbearing. Just because our motif "under the sea," it doesn't mean that we should be eating salmon and have squid in our punch.

This being my first prom, it comes as a bit of a surprise. The only other dances I've attended have been loud, junior high affairs or poorly orchestrated homecoming events. My expectations, therefore, were fairly low. To my surprise, prom is, well, classy. There is still a bit of the sitting on the sides of the dance floor from junior high, but this time the students are sitting on tables covered with fine linens. Obviously there is music, but it's not the blaring, annoying crap that I've heard at other dances. It's tasteful and not obscenely loud.

"Do you want to dance right away?" she asks. Oh yes, the dancing.

"Let's stake out a table first," I reply, merely trying to postpone the inevitable. I see Scott and his date, Samantha, nearby and we make our way over to them. Samantha was a last-minute choice for Scott, and he insists they're just here as friends. That may be true, but I think something might develop from it. We'll see. Sam has gone with a dress that nearly engulfs the chair she's sitting on. Scott, like me, is in a black tux. "Hey Scott," I say when we get over to them, "We're kind of at a disadvantage here."

"Yeah?" he replies, "Why is that?"

"Look around. There are about 100 girls here, all with different hairstyles and different dresses of different colors. There are also 100 guys here, all wearing the same black tuxedo and all having one of maybe a dozen different hairstyles. We're boring."

"Not that boring," he says, nodding toward the door. I turn to look, and in walks Jimmy Mehr, a virtual nobody in Milaca. He is dressed in a white tuxedo and a top hat. With him is a stunningly beautiful girl who I've never seen before in my life. Trust me, I would have remembered. She's wearing a low-cut black dress and stiletto heels, and she walks in like she owns the place.

"Wow," Scott says. Sam elbows him in the ribs.

"Who is that, his sister?" I ask no one in particular.

"No," Scott answers, "There's no way they're from the same gene pool. I don't know what happened to Mehr. It's like he's a whole different person."

"Wait a minute, look at the guy's shoes," I say, pointing to Jimmy's pearly white wingtips. "Don't they belong to Bish?"

Sara nods, "I've seen him wear them. Why?" I look around the ballroom until I see Bish leaning up against one wall. I catch his eye.

"Another project?" I mouth. He smiles and gives a short, simple nod. I should have known.

The dance goes swimmingly. Sara and I talk, we have our picture taken, and we even dance. At first I was just going to take part in the slow songs, leaving the rest to people who could, well, dance. Eventually I let Sara drag me onto the floor, and believe it or not, I actually have fun. I'm sure I look like an idiot to the untrained observer, but I have a good time. Before I know it, it's time for the last dance of the night. I wrap my arms around Sara and we dance, rocking back and forth to the music.

"Thank you," she softly whispers into my ear.

"For what?"

"For making prom wonderful," she replies, pulling me closer.

I smile. "Wait 'til you see what's next."

Bish pulls the big black car up to the house and kills the engine.

"Sir, we have arrived," he says, opening my door.

"Where are we?" Sara asks as she gets out. Bish ignores her.

"Your packages," he says, handing me two duffel bags. "Regrettably, I have some further business to attend to elsewhere. I trust you will be able to find your way home safely."

"Yes. Thank you Jeeves," I tell him.

"Certainly, sir." With that Bish strolls over to his Mustang, fires it up, and thunders down the driveway.

"Ok, what is all this?" Sara asks, apparently suspicious of the whole ordeal. "Where are we? Whose house is this?"

"Relax," I reply. "We're just going for a swim."

"What?! It's freezing outside!"

"That is why man invented hot tubs." She doesn't seem totally convinced.

"I'm not swimming in my prom dress," she says, "And I'm not going to run around naked in someone else's backyard." I knew the skinny dipping thing wouldn't work out.

"Not so fast," I say, pulling out her suit. Regrettably, it's a one-piece. "Follow me." I lead her around to the back of the house. "You can change in there," I say, pointing to a small shed built for the same purpose. She tries to talk, but I stop her with a kiss. "Ah ah, shut up. You don't get to talk now. Go." She pouts for a second, but then flashes a smile.

"Whatever you say."

As she goes off to change, I open the duffel bag and finish unpacking. I lay out a handful of towels, some fruit juices, and some choco-late-covered strawberries. I take care to make sure that everything is set up correctly, even arranging the strawberries in a perfect circle. I look up when I hear Sara come out of the changing room, and then I realize our prom night will go even better than I expected.

CHAPTER 74

I spend most of Sunday in bed, catching up on my lost sleep. I'm sure that it will throw my schedule out of whack; we didn't get home until slightly before dawn, but it really doesn't matter. Saturday night was well worth it.

At school on Monday everyone is talking about prom. Who went where with who, who got drunk where, who was busted by the cops, everything seems to be open for discussion. I try to find Sara before first hour to see what she thought of the evening, but she's nowhere to be found. She finally walks into chemistry just before the bell rings. Instead of going straight to her seat, she walks over to me first.

"Thank you," she whispers in my ear. I smile. I guess that's the answer I was looking for.

The rest of the day is spent planning for the cabin shindig next weekend. Helga and Hagar are actually letting me have a decent-sized gathering with my friends. I think its good timing, I've been alienating my friends a little bit since Sara and I have been involved. It's not entirely my fault, there are only so many hours in a day, but I still feel guilty about it. I'd call the gathering this weekend a party, but that always seems to conjure up images of loud music and lots of people I don't know, so this weekend's brouhaha shall be deemed "Cabin Shindig." If things go smoothly it should be a grand 'ol time.

The week goes amazingly well. I don't have to work on Wednesday, so Sara and I go out for a picnic in the park. We mess around, play on the jungle gym, and even get to play on the swings. In the midst of running around I find myself kissing her in one of the little playhouses at the top of a slide. We stay up there for quite some time. It isn't until I get home that I realize that without Sara I would probably doing the same things with Allison. Well, without the smooching.

Sara and I get together again on Thursday night to watch a movie at my house. It's strange, I used to be disgusted when I would see little freshmen couples kissing in the school hallways. Now it seems that I have become much less judgmental, probably because now I see what I've been missing.

CHAPTER 75

By the time Saturday rolls around and all of the RSVPs are counted, I've got seven coming for the shindig. Scott, Bish and Sara are all on the guest list, as are Allison, Richard, Aaron, and Pete. Adam couldn't come because he's working, slogging away at a cabinet shop to make $7.50 an hour. Poor kid. A few others couldn't come for various reasons, but for the most part everyone who I really wanted to have up is coming.

My morning is spent setting everything out for the event. I considered letting everyone follow me up to the lake, but I decided to just give everyone a map and hope they have the sense to follow it. If someone can't figure out how to read a map, then they're not smart enough to be my friend. The food for the event is relatively simple; chips, dip, and sandwiches make up the bulk of the meals, supplemented by a pan of my world-famous brownies. Ok fine, they're Betty Crocker's world-famous brownies, but nobody needs to know. I rig the sailboat too. The water's still pretty cold, but a few hearty souls might be up for it.

The first guests show up at about ten or so. Scott arrives first, as expected. There's little fear of being the first one at a party when your best friend is hosting it. I don't bother to go out to meet him and he doesn't bother to knock.

"Need any help?" he asks.

"Not here," I reply, dropping the last of the soda cans into the cooler. "I could use a hand setting up the volleyball net though." He follows me outside and we go about untangling the jumbled net. The next time I put it away I should realize that I'll probably be the next one to set it up.

"So who's all coming?" he asks.

"The final list includes you, Bish, Sara, Al, Richard, Aaron, and Pete. I tried to get Sam to come, but she said she has something going on."

"Yeah," he replies, "She had to go down to Morris for her cousin's wedding."

"How are things going with her these days?"

"Pretty good, I guess."

"Are you two dating?"

He smiles, "Not yet. How are things going with Sara?" I reply with a wide grin. Scott shakes his head. "Silly me. Why did I even bother to ask?"

The rest of the crowd arrives in due time. Once all the cars are parked and all the backpacks are brought in, everyone assembles in the living room.

"So now what?" Aaron asks.

"I don't know," I ay, "What do you guys want to do?"

"Let's all go swimming!" Allison suggests.

"No way," Richard replies. "At this time of the year the water is in the low forties. Comfortable swimming temperatures are around eighty degrees. Right now you wouldn't just be cold, you would probably succumb to hypothermia within fifteen to twenty-five minutes."

"Oh," she says.

Scott speaks up. "Well, we've already got the volleyball net up, and we've got enough people to play a game. Why don't we do that?" No one objects. As we walk out to the court we form up teams, trying to get them as even as we can. It shakes out to be me, Allison, Richard, and Pete against Bish, Scott, Aaron, and Sara. One might think that it would be best for me to play on the same team as my best friend and my girlfriend, but that couldn't be farther from the truth. If we're against each other a bit of taunting is more than likely, but we probably won't yell at each other for missing a block or botching a spike. I wouldn't want anything to get in the way of smooches. (From Sara. Not Scott.)

"You guys are goin' down Larkin!" Aaron yells.

"Go ahead, keep talking," I reply, picking up the ball. "You'll be eating your words in a minute."

The game itself is surprisingly well played. For some reason I seem to be gifted with friends who have the ability to play volleyball. The biggest surprise is Bish. Despite the fact that he has never been in any high school sport whatsoever, he's all over the court. When we're finished I ask him about his newfound talents.

"Bish, where did that all come from?" I ask.

"Whatever do you mean?"

I roll my eyes, "That," I say, pointing at the court. "You were out there kicking ass and taking names. Where did all that come from?"

He shrugs. "I participate in a bit of semi-professional ball in the summer months."

"Semi-pro volleyball?"

Bish smiles, "One's life cannot be completely devoid of physical activity." Then he walks away as I try to wrap my mind around the concept of Bishop playing volleyball in swim trunks and sunglasses. Weird.

After the game we hunt down some lunch, descending on the kitchen like locusts. I am appalled by the actions of my mother. There isn't a breath of "clean up your mess" or "take out the garbage." There's just "I'll get it" and "no problem." Double weird. Maybe she's trying to lay a guilt trip on me, or maybe she's just being nice. I wish I could discern this stuff.

"So what do you guys want to do now?" I ask.

"Go swimming!" Al says.

"No, seriously."

"Seriously!" she says, digging out her swimsuit. "I'm going swimming. Anyone who'd like to join me is more than welcome." No one moves. "Fine."

"Wait," I say, standing up. "I'll go."

"Why?" Sara asks. "You'll freeze."

"I'll be fine," I reply, shrugging her off. "Besides, I've never been out quite this early. It'll be a new personal record for me."

Aaron sighs and stands up, "I guess I'm in too."

"Good." Al says. "Anyone else? Scott?"

He shakes his head. "No way."

"I suppose I would be up to the challenge," Bish says.

Al makes one more pass around the room. "Anyone else?" No one else stands up. "All right then, let's go."

Once we're changed and ready to go the eight of us march down to the docks. The four swimmers, including myself, are all sure to bring extra towels for when we get out of the water.

"How long do you think they'll last?" Aaron asks Scott.

Scott shrugs. "It's hard to tell. If it was me I'd be getting out as fast as I can, but with these guys it's hard to tell."

"So how are we going to do this?" Aaron asks, looking nervously at the water. "Are we all going to jump in at once?"

"It would be the most logical course of action," Bish says. "There may be a mad rush for the dock once we are in the water, but I fear that if we go in individually someone may be prone to dropping out."

"All right," I say, "We'll all go in at once." The non-swimmers back away, making sure they're clear of the imminent splash. We shed our towels and stand on the edge of the dock, periodically looking over our shoulders to make sure no one is running up to push us in. "Everybody ready?" I'm answered with a few short nods. I realize that I'll want to prevent anyone from dropping out now, the wusses. "And remember," I add, "If you hesitate and don't jump you'll still get hit by the splash. Now on three. One…two…THREE!"

I jump to the side as much as I do forward, not wanting to land on anyone or have them land on me. When I hit the water it takes my breath away. I go numb immediately, and the initial shock is enough to send me rocketing back to the top of the water. When I hit the surface I hear Aaron howling.

"MY GOD THAT'S COLD!" he yells. The water is quickly numbing my entire body to the point where it's painful, and I start to swim for the dock. I drag myself up onto the dock and grab a towel. I'm starting to re-think my decision to get out. Now that I'm wet the air feels even colder than the water.

"How's the water?" Scott asks.

"Shaddup," Aaron snaps, snatching a towel from him. Allison is well on her way to warming up as well, she's already thrown on a sweatshirt that she was smart enough to bring with. That's when I realize that Bish is missing from the dock.

"Where's Bish?" I ask, spinning around. He's not in the water either. "BISH!" Then everyone else joins in.

"Bishop!"

"Bish, are you ok?"

"Should I jump in after him?" I ask.

"There will be no need for that," a voice says.

"Bish, is that you?" I say, looking around one more time.

"Quite right." I still can't see him.

"Where are you?"

"Right here," he says. Soon after a wave of icy water shoots up from under me. I jump up, then look down to see Bish, calmly treading water under the dock.

"Hello," he says.

"Christ man," says Aaron. "Richard was right; the water is freezing. What the hell are you doing?"

"It's all a matter of willpower, really," comes the reply. "I'm merely following the Zen practice of mind over body."

"Fine by me," I say, heading for the cabin. "But this body is due for a hot shower."

Once the four of us are showered and changed, the group breaks up a bit. The girls go for a walk, Aaron and Pete decide to hurl rocks into the lake, and Scott, Bish, Richard, and I retire to the porch for a vicious game of Scrabble. The evening ends with smores around the campfire. Looking around the fire at the faces of my friends, I realize how nice it is to have them here. I don't know what I'd do without them.

CHAPTER 76

"Come on Fatty McGee," Aaron yells at me as he charges up a hill. Aaron, Pete, and I managed to get together to go mountain biking today. We usually don't get a chance to ride together during the week, but for some reason things worked out for this afternoon.

"Shut up, ass." I reply, dragging myself behind him. My mind knows that I should work to become a better climber, but my body goes into it kicking and screaming. Mostly screaming.

"I never got a chance to ask," Pete says, coming up behind me. "How did prom night with Sara go?"

"Wonderful," I yell back over my shoulder. "I don't know how things could have gone better."

"Wow," he replies. "Not too shabby then. Did you get some ass?"

"Maybe. It's not all a bed of roses though," I add. "She's been really busy this week and I've hardly been able to talk to her." I think for a second. "On and unrelated side note, I wouldn't think a bed of roses would be all that comfortable. They're pretty damn thorny." The guys laugh. "Aaron, is Pete still after the little tikes?"

"What are you talking about?" Pete asks.

I explain. "Well, I heard you were chasing seventh and eighth graders; how did all of that turn out?"

"Actually," Aaron says, pulling off to the side of the trail at the top of a hill, "From what I've heard Pete has given all of that up."

"I have," Pete says, pulling up beside us. "It wasn't really worth it."

"Why?" I ask.

"Well, they're not quite as mature as girls my own age."

"Wait a second." I say, "When have you ever been worried about maturity when it comes to girls?"

Pete smiles. "I mean the older ones are more mature physically."

I nod. "Now that makes sense." Now rested, we drop down the hill and back into the trail system. "Have you guys ever wondered what the perfect girl would be like?"

Aaron looks over his shoulder, "You mean Sara isn't the perfect girl?"

"Not quite," I reply. "She doesn't have a British accent."

"A British accent?"

"Yeah, I've always thought of them as being exceptionally attractive."

"No way," he replies. "I don't think I could take my date saying 'Blimey!' when she spills water on her dress." The kid has a point.

Another half an hour finds us by the side of the trail once more, this time not by choice.

"God I hate doing this," I say, working my tire off the rim.

"Then you should quit getting flats," Aaron replies, leaning up against a nearby tree. I finally work the tube out of the rim and go about patching it. I've acquired more than my fair share of flats in the past few years, and patching them has gotten to be a familiar practice. My front tube is starting to look like a quilt.

"So what do you guys think I should do for Sara before she flies out?" I ask.

"Where's she going again?" Pete asks.

"She's off to Europe for a few weeks, and I want to do something special for her."

"What about a mix tape of her favorite songs?" Aaron suggests.

"A mix tape? A mix tape is something the druggies put together between bong hits, not something you give your girlfriend before she goes away for a month."

"You could give her roses. All girls like roses," Pete says.

"Too cliché," I reply, "Besides, I've done it before."

"Ok, I've got it," Pete says. "A sauna and a hot oil massage."

"You know what?" I say, finishing with the tire, "I probably shouldn't have asked. I'll take care of it myself."

"Do you have something cooked up?" Aaron asks, climbing back onto his bike.

I smile. "Yeah, I've got a few ideas."

CHAPTER 77

"It's strange to think that you're leaving tomorrow," I say, driving down the streets of Milaca. Sara sits next to me, watching the town slide by.

"I know," she says. "The idea that in twenty-four hours I'll be thousands and thousands of miles away is weird."

"You fly out at ten, right?"

She nods. "Why?"

I smile, "I thought I might come down to see you off."

"Will, you don't have to do that."

I nod. "I know."

"Where are we going, anyway?" she asks.

"Can't tell you."

"Come on," she pleads, "Just a hint?"

"Nope. Besides, we're almost there."

A few minutes later we pull up to Bakersfield Park, a small collection of softball fields nested down by the river.

"What are we doing here?" Sara asks.

"You'll see." I get out of the car and walk around to open her door.

"You know, it's pretty hard to play softball in the dark," she says, getting out of the car. I don't reply. Taking her hand, I lead her across the darkened field toward a small point of light. "What is that?" she asks.

I shrug. "I don't want you to go stumbling over things in the dark." As we get closer the pinpoint materializes into a bamboo torch planted alongside a narrow trail.

"What is all this?"

"Follow me and you'll find out," I reply. I grab the torch and lead her down the path. As we sink deeper into the forest fairies seem to flicker and fade in front of us. When we get closer they don't fade, but resolve into candles of all shapes and sizes lining the trail, bathing the forest in their soft glow.

"Oh my God," she says. I plant the torch in the ground and continue without it, relying on the candles to light my way. When I reach the end of the path I turn to see Sara picking her way down the trail, glowing with candlelight. I can't remember when I've seen anything like it.

"Where are we?" she asks, looking around. I turn to reveal a long dock behind me, reaching out over the river. It too is strung with candles, ending with a blanket and a picnic basket on the far end.

"It's so beautiful," she says.

"Come on," I say, let's go sit down. I lead her along the dock. The glassy river reflects both the candles and the stars, making it feel like we're entering another world. Sara sits down on one of the blankets and looks back upon the forest, which is alight with dancing pixies and fairies.

"There are grapes and juice in the picnic basket," I say, sitting next to her. Sara doesn't reply, she just pulls me close and kisses me. "What was that for?"

"Thank you," she replies, "For everything."

"No problem."

"No," she says, taking my head in her hands. "For everything. Thanks for putting up with me." I see. We're not just talking about the candles.

"You know what?" I say, "It was worth it. Come here." I pull her close and we lie back to look at the stars. "About all of this; you're going away tomorrow and I wanted to give you a night to remember here at home. I don't want you running off with some Italian guy and forgetting all about me."

"Oh, there's no worry about that," she says. "Trust me."

"What, you've tried it?"

"You bet I have."

"You ran away with some Italian guy?"

She rolls on her side to face me. "No, I tried to forget you. The whole time I was with Dave I tried to ignore you, but I just couldn't do it. I thought I might have to kill Julie." No way. The odds were %100 the whole time and I had no idea. God I'm an idiot.

"Why didn't you say anything?" I ask.

She smiles, "Because I didn't know what I was missing." She slides closer to me and kisses me once, then twice. Then, well, have you ever heard the song "Behind Closed Doors?" It's a good song.

CHAPTER 78

Seeing Sara at off the airport ends up to be one of the harder things I've ever done. I know it's stupid; I'll see her in a few weeks, but I can't help but feel like I'm losing her. I ride to the airport with Sara and her parents and we follow her to the gate. She says her goodbyes to her folks, and then her parents do one of the nicest things anyone has ever done for me: they go away. This allows us to say our goodbyes.

"I can't believe you're leaving. It seems so soon," I say, holding her tight.

"I know, I don't want to go, especially after last night."

"Quit it," I say, pulling back a little. "The trip will be great."

"Now boarding, rows twenty through thirty-nine," blares a loud-speaker nearby.

"That's me," she says, pulling me close. "I'll miss you."

"I'll miss you too." We kiss. "You'll write me?"

"Every day," she says. She checks over her shoulder. "I've got to go."

"Go," kiss, "Have fun," kiss, "And write," another kiss.

"I will. Goodbye Will."

"Bye."

The girl of my dreams grabs her backpack and walks quickly to the gate. The attendant checks her ticket, and just before she heads down the jetway Sara turns to give me one last wave. I wave back, doing my best to smile, but fighting back tears. She turns down the jetway and disappears from my sight.

I work my way to a huge window facing the plane as it's prepared for departure. That's my girlfriend out there, and I hope to God she comes back safe. If she doesn't, God will have some tough questions to answer.

"I hate goodbyes," says a voice to my right. I turn to see a girl, about my age, staring out the window.

"I know what you mean," I reply. "Boyfriend?"

"I wish." She turns to face me. "No, it's my brother. He's going off to college." Once she turns and I get a good look at her, I'm stunned. She's gorgeous. Not in the traditional sense, but her deep green eyes, her face framed with short chestnut hair, the way her body fits so perfectly into her jeans and blue t-shirt, everything stuns me. "Hi," she says. "I'm Kelly." I reach out and shake her angelic hand.

"I'm Will."

THE END

About the Author

Born in 1984, Jacob Vos is just beginning to break into the ranks of distinguished authors. A graduate of the Milaca High School Class of 2002, he plans to go on to St. John's University. As an author and a poet, he has had a number of pieces published in anthologies such as Teen Ink and Twilight Remembrances, but this is his first full-length novel. He is also an actor, performing in a number of plays, including Our Town, A Midsummer Night's Dream, McBeth, Sweeny Todd, The Potman Spoke Sooth, Why Do We Laugh, and The Laramie Project. He has been awarded both Best Actor (Our Town, Why Do We Laugh) and Best Supporting Actor (Sweeney Todd).

0-595-21974-8